DANEY PARKER

Copyright © 2025 by Daney Parker
All rights reserved.

ISBN: 979-8312278156

No part of this book may be reproduced in any form or by any electronic or mechanical means, including information storage and retrieval systems, without written permission from the author, except for the use of brief quotations in a book review.

For Lyra and Ellis

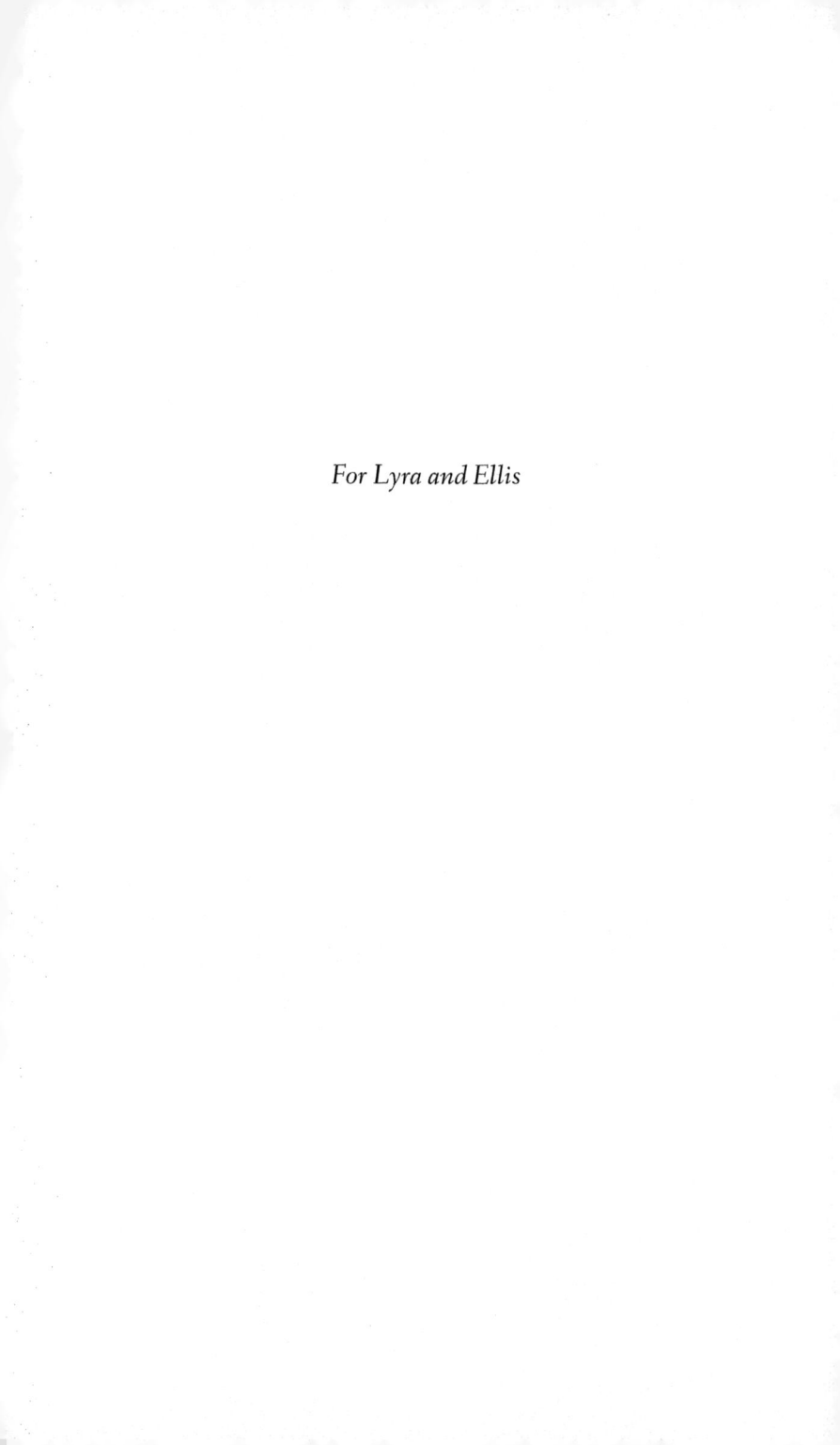

Contents

About the Author	vii
Also by Daney Parker	ix
Prologue	1
Chapter One	3
Chapter Two	5
Chapter Three	15
Chapter Four	25
Chapter Five	27
Chapter Six	38
Chapter Seven	49
Chapter Eight	52
Chapter Nine	61
Chapter Ten	65
Chapter Eleven	70
Chapter Twelve	75
Chapter Thirteen	83
Chapter Fourteen	93
Chapter Fifteen	100
Chapter Sixteen	103
Chapter Seventeen	110
Chapter Eighteen	115
Chapter Nineteen	122
Chapter Twenty	127
Chapter Twenty-One	132
Chapter Twenty-Two	138
Chapter Twenty-Three	141
Chapter Twenty-Four	145
Chapter Twenty-Five	151
Chapter Twenty-Six	157
Chapter Twenty-Seven	164

Chapter Twenty-Eight	167
Chapter Twenty-Nine	173
Epilogue	178
Acknowledgments	185

About the Author

Daney Parker has loved working with words for as long as she can remember. She is delighted that she has managed to make a living following her passion – copywriting, publishing in magazines and now writing domestic thrillers. As well as writing, Daney likes to chat... she is particularly good at asking probing questions, getting people to confess their deepest, darkest secrets. So if you ever meet up with her, be careful what you reveal. She writes overlooking the sea in the Isle of Wight.

Daney's debut novel The Push Over was shortlisted for the Ink Book fiction prize. You can read further musings and updates about work in progress at www.daneyparker.co.uk

Also by Daney Parker

The Push Over, shortlisted for the Ink Book Fiction Prize 2024.

Prologue
October 2020

Laura

A twilight gloom drains the colour from the garden, the air dense and still. The birds are silent, as if they know it would be disrespectful to sing. There is nothing to be happy about here.

When we get to the front door, I can't open it because my hands have become useless, refusing to follow my brain's commands, so I pass the key to Henry. We walk into the hallway and Henry steers me to the stairs where I collapse, my head between my knees.

"Stay here," he says. "I'll look around."

I hear Henry's footsteps on the hardwood hall floor, doors being opened, then silence as he steps into carpeted rooms. He moves past me up the stairs. There is a loud noise, which sounds like a door being forced open. This is followed by nothing. I strain to catch any sound, but there is only silence. Eventually I hear Henry's voice, although I can't make out what he is saying. More footsteps, and then I watch Henry come slowly down the stairs, his expression blank, face drained of blood. He looks like a bad waxwork of himself.

"He is in his bathroom on the floor. I have called for an ambulance," he says. "I couldn't find a pulse. There is no breath, but his body is not cold. We might have been able to save him if we had come earlier."

I feel a huge wave of relief wash over me. "Well, thank God we didn't get here any earlier then."

That prompts our hysteria. Uncontrollable laughter engulfs both of us, as if our bodies are trying to shake off all the stress of the last six months. We are both soon gasping for air, the pain of the convulsions of our bodies almost too hard to bear.

The doorbell rings and we let in the two ambulance people – one man, reassuringly large and bearlike, the other a woman, also a solid and significant presence. Exactly the sort of people you want to have around you in a crisis. I indicate upstairs. "My dad is on the floor in the ..." At last, the appropriate types of tears arrive.

The bear says, "Stay here, we will check on him."

We hear no sounds of attempted resuscitation, so maybe the death was longer ago than Henry thinks. Then the woman appears and comes down the stairs. She moves as if to put her latex-gloved hand on my shoulder, then quickly pulls it back.

Touching strangers, even to comfort them, has stopped being an option since March.

She says, "I am so sorry, there was nothing we could do. Your father is dead."

Chapter One

First sign of a psychopath: ability to exaggerate the truth to get their way

Henry

Mission accomplished. I sit in silence with Laura in the car for a few moments, before I turn the ignition key and we drive home. As I put my foot down on the accelerator, I feel a familiar pain shoot up my right leg. Sciatica. My constant companion.

I don't turn on the radio; our thoughts are loud enough to keep our brains busy. I have been preparing for this and now, at last, I can put everything in motion. Except something feels wrong.

Is it guilt? Brian deserved to die, and anyway, I was a bystander. It wasn't my idea, although I encouraged it. My act at the end was an act of kindness, but it is just as well there were no witnesses.

No, I must keep my resolve. An old Clash song starts

playing inside my head, the same few lines on repeat: *"Should I stay or should I go now? If I go, there will be trouble. And if I stay it will be double."*

Chapter Two

Second sign of a psychopath: huge sense of
self-importance

Laura

The path to committing murder is crooked and paved with bad intentions. Like many paths, you begin not knowing where you will end up; you just take one step at a time. Eventually you discover where it is taking you, but carry on regardless.

When I was small, I thought it strange how much other kids clearly loved their dads; I thought there must be something wrong with me. Dad sometimes asked me why I didn't run to him and throw my arms around him when he got home from work, like kids were supposed to. Far from feeling happy when I heard his key in the lock in the evening, I would hide myself away, dreading him finding me. Luckily, he never looked for me – I don't know what I thought he would do if he should find me. Really, what a strange child I was!

Why didn't I adore Dad? Surely it is the default in young children to adore their parents? It is easy to see Dad's faults now, but I can't pinpoint anything he did when I was young that made me hate him as much as I did.

I flick through early memories and settle on what we used to do regularly on Sunday afternoons. We would all be in the first-floor living room of our four-bedroomed town house on Richmond Hill, which my mother had inherited (I think this was what mainly attracted Dad to her). Dad would play with his motor-racing Scalextric track. This toy was bought for me, he claimed, but I was not allowed to touch it in case I broke it. He would spend hours racing his miniature cars. He insisted my mother and I stay with him as he played, as it was no fun to play games on your own. My mum would be with me in the corner of the room, she was perched on a bar stool. She had wonderful poise, gained from her finishing school in Switzerland.

I sprawled on the wooden parquet floor, surrounded by colouring books and dry felt tip pens that scratched the pictures more than they coloured them in, whilst Mum called up friends and sipped cocktails. Gulping cocktails may be a more accurate way of describing my mum's drinking, as her drinks disappeared in the blink of an eye. Luckily, her bar stool was next to the bar – such a "cool feature", as she often exclaimed – so she got regular top-ups.

I carry on going through the Rolodex of my past, trying to find a particularly unhappy recollection, or even a happy one, of being with my father, but none appear. He never abused me physically. Okay, sometimes he would grab my arm so tightly that afterwards there would be a dark bruise, but he didn't slap me – nowhere as near as often as Mum did anyway. It was acceptable to hit kids in the seventies. I know other people have had far worse childhoods than

Chapter Two

mine, and they don't end up killing their parents. Maybe the world would be a better place if they did.

Like probably many other malcontents, I had nasty fantasies from an unseasonably young age. All of these were about making my dad disappear.

When I was at junior school, my friend Lucy used to tell me off for being grumpy around my dad when she came over for a play-date. All she could see was Dad being charming. He could be suave, especially to pretty girls, and Lucy was terribly pretty. And slim. "Why are you always so mean to your dad? You never say anything nice to him, and he's great. So funny!"

I learnt to stay silent about how I felt; other kids just wouldn't get it. So all the bizarre hatred I felt for Dad festered. For years, those bad thoughts flourished in the enclosed environment of my imagination, well-fed by self-pity, resentment, and disappointment.

It wasn't until I married Henry that I felt safe enough to expose the rottenness of my feelings, and instead of stamping on my dreams about murdering my father, Henry positively nurtured them.

Eventually I do the unforgivable. I take an action that crosses the line. An action that could make me a murderer. It is March 2020; the country has just gone into lockdown. My dad is eighty-five and takes tablets for high blood pressure, plus he claims he had a heart attack after a cocaine-fuelled orgy in New York (one of his favourite anecdotes, best not to ask), so I think it is likely he will not survive getting COVID-19.

The news is full of how only people with underlying

health conditions are at risk, and that young people never get it badly. When I hear George, our youngest, coughing, I'm not worried at all. Instead, I start making plans.

George has just returned from his first year at uni – there's nothing to do in Newcastle, he says, and he can work better at home. Daisy has also returned from her student house in Nottingham, so we have a full house. George says he is not feeling poorly at all, that I'm worrying too much about him. He says he has looked up all the symptoms online of COVID-19, and according to the NHS guidance he doesn't have it and is safe to lead his life as normal. He has no temperature and his cough is the wrong sort as it isn't a dry cough. He is convinced he just has a mild cold.

Meanwhile, Dad is self-isolating, despite all his proclamations that he is lonely on his own. I persuaded him that he had no choice, that I would get all his food for him, and that I would regularly pop in to check up on him. I always make an effort to appear to be nice to Dad, say all the things he wants to hear, and also pander to his demands. I find it easier to handle him that way.

I ask George if he can cook a stew, his signature dish, for us both to take to his grandfather. George says he would rather not, as it's "hardly a fun trip out".

Dad has never been nice to George. He resents both our children because they take my attention away from him. As our kids have grown up, he has never had a good word to say about them, apart from making inappropriate remarks about Daisy's appearance. I remember him saying she had a "sexy wiggle" when she was about ten, and although I told him he really shouldn't say stuff like that, he hasn't stopped. Whenever I complain, he says I'm just jealous because I was such an unappealing child.

When I explain to George that he should come and visit

Chapter Two

Dad because it gives us a chance to infect him, George's mouth opens wide, but he can't find the words and for a while he is speechless. Not like him at all. As much as George dislikes visiting his grandfather, he obviously isn't happy about my suggestion to give the old man COVID. "I'm not a psychopath like you," he eventually says.

He does agree to come, but "only because I know I haven't got the virus, and also to help you out, as I know grandad always upsets you. One of my friends whose dad is a virologist says that having a cold could protect you from COVID, as it is a coronavirus too, so you build up antibodies. So despite your nasty plans to knock off your dad, I would actually be doing him a favour by giving him what I've got ..."

Even if what George is saying is true – which I doubt, as he is always full of misinformation gathered from the internet and his friends – I decide that it is worth taking George to see Dad. As well as not trusting George's theories, I don't trust all the information the government is putting out right now. I think everyone who has any symptoms at all should be isolating. I know I tend to think that every cough and cold the kids have could be the sign of something worse, but this time I reckon it is very possible that George does have COVID-19.

George and I go to my father's house with a casserole dish of vegetable stew and stuff I grabbed at random from Waitrose. I know Dad will not notice that George is not looking his healthiest and wouldn't dream of asking us about ourselves, so the subject of passing on the virus should not come up.

George gets into the spirit of his mission to improve Dad's immune system by giving him a big hug as soon as he opens the front door. Dad has a look of horror on his face.

"No need for you to get all touchy feely," he says as he pushes George away.

I wonder if he suspects George is gay, as he hates homosexuals. Although it would be out of character for him to actually notice something about George – usually he takes in no information about anyone else. Even now, after over thirty years, he often can't remember Henry's name, calling him "your husband", and he gets the kids' names wrong too.

Dad has always had a thing about gay men, disliking them almost as much as he dislikes foreigners. He himself has a dark olive complexion, which means people are always asking him where he is from "originally". This question sends him into a rage as he explains he is from Richmond. When people then ask where his parents are from, they are lucky not to get punched, but Dad contains his fury and says through gritted teeth that his parents were both Londoners. People generally feel the waves of anger emanating from Dad at this point and stop this line of enquiry.

Dad's mum had a bit of a reputation in her day. She was the talk of the neighbourhood because she had so many affairs, which could explain why Dad is so dark. I remember when we covered genetics in biology, I was puzzled because my textbook claimed that two blue-eyed people could not have a brown-eyed child, as blue eyes are a recessive gene. Both my grandparents on my dad's side had blue eyes, whereas Dad and his sister have dark, dark brown eyes. This suggests that my grandfather is not genetically their father, which makes sense, as my grandmother was so often unfaithful. Although it is surprising she had an affair with the same man long enough to conceive both her children, who were born ten years apart. Another, more feasible

Chapter Two

explanation is that she had more than one fling with a dark-brown-eyed man.

When Dad sees the stew, he asks who made it. When George claims the honours, Dad says, "Well I had better wait until I'm really hungry to try this then." He isn't joking; he probably thinks he is at risk of catching homosexuality from the food, despite his physical resilience that he likes to boast about.

As he unpacks the shopping, Dad makes little grunts of disapproval. It's clear I have chosen all the things he doesn't like. He asks how much I paid for the smoked salmon and tells me I wasted my money. Why hadn't I gone to the supermarket just before it closed and got some bargains?

"At least I haven't wasted my money on all this fancy stuff. You've always been awful with money – that's why I never trusted you with pocket money." Dad also used this excuse as justification for not paying towards my grant when I was at university, or for ever giving me money. "It is just as well you're overpaid for that boring job you do, the amount you fritter away."

Whilst we are in the kitchen, Dad's phone rings. He takes it out of his pocket and looks furious when he sees the screen.

"I'll just take this," he says as he hurries out of the room. He starts talking, or rather shouting, into it after he has slammed the kitchen door shut and we hear him scream: "This is the last bloody time!"

He comes back, looking flushed.

"Who was that, Dad?" I ask

"Just a nuisance call."

I have told Dad numerous times how he can get himself off many of the lists of spam callers, but he always ignores me. I have never known anyone get as many junk calls as he gets. Whenever I'm with him, I guarantee that he will get at least one.

"Grandad," George says, "if you give me your phone I can help you stop getting those calls if you like."

"Oh don't you start!" Dad shouts. "I get this enough from your mother!"

I think it is time to go.

After we leave Dad's house I sit in the car and rest my head on the steering wheel and count to twenty. I always felt wiped out after seeing him. As I regain my composure, George says what a drama queen I am for making out I have been through some sort of traumatic event. "Why do you let him get to you? He is just a boring, self-obsessed old git. Like lots of old men. You should have therapy or something – it's crazy that you react like this all the time. Grandad could live to at least a hundred. You don't want visiting him to ruin the last few years of your life."

"I think I have more than just a few years left thanks, George," I say as we drive off.

"If you carry on like this, you'll end up giving yourself a stroke. Then Grandad will outlive you."

That is what I have always been afraid of – that I won't have any years on this planet without my dad tainting them. This is one of the reasons why he has to go. Soon.

Three days later, I'm in bed with a temperature. A day after this, Henry takes to the bed in the spare room, also feverish. Our coughs, which unlike George's are barking and dry, resonate through the house. George is now completely better and claims we must have got the virus from someone

Chapter Two

else, as he definitely has not had anything like what we've got. Daisy is fine, too.

Just as well the children are home and healthy, as Henry and I aren't up to looking after ourselves. Lucky that I stocked up on the basics, including plenty of tins of soup, before we got ill. Our house is now in quarantine.

After a few more days, I'm feeling weak, but the fever is gone. The cough is irritating, but not too debilitating. It is such a relief to wake up and actually be able to get out of bed. Everyone else is still asleep as I make myself a cup of coffee. The first coffee I have had in days. I sniff the jar, looking forward to its familiar, comforting aroma. Nothing. I must have lost my sense of smell.

As I sit at the kitchen table, cradling the warm mug of tasteless coffee in my hands, the phone rings. Dad.

"I feel awful. I've been up all night. I'm burning up ... It feels like there is no air in the room. I think you should come over right now and take my temperature. See if I need to call the doctor.

"Oh no, poor Dad!" I say. "I'm ill too, or I would come over. Have you got paracetamol? I think *you* should call the doctor!"

"You don't sound ill to me. Come over now, or send one of your kids."

"They are still asleep ..."

"You spoil them. You should think of me for a change. If it weren't for me, looking after you and giving you all those night feeds when you were a baby, you wouldn't be here now." Dad likes to remind me that because my mum was so unwell after my birth, he had to look after me for a few weeks on his own. He used to say: "You took so long taking your bloody bottle that I wanted to throw you out the window." He thought he was a saint for not murdering me, as I was such a needy baby.

"I'm sorry, Dad, but I can't come. You know how I am about rules. Try taking some paracetamol to start off with and if that doesn't help, maybe call 111?"

Dad doesn't have paracetamol, as such, but finds some Lemsips in the house. He says he will make one for himself and go straight back to bed. I ask him to call me the minute he wakes up, and that I will call for an ambulance if he doesn't call or if his symptoms get worse.

His symptoms do not get worse. Four days later he is shouting down the phone as loudly as ever.

This is when I realise it is going to take quite a lot to take Dad down. He has the constitution of an ox. As much as I would like to beat him to death with a shovel sometimes, I do not have the strength, and I know I would never get away with it.

I will have to put some real thought into it, and come up with a viable plan.

Chapter Three

Third sign of a psychopath: craving unlimited
success, power, brilliance, beauty

Laura

There are nearly ten thousand recorded COVID deaths in the UK. All four of us, plus Jeff the Dog, are now stuck at home in week two of lockdown. I am the only one earning right now, doing accounts for local businesses. Henry is working on his novel, and the kids are mostly in their rooms doing course work, or so they claim. Whenever I go past their bedrooms, all I can hear is loud chatting and laughter – both of them are on permanent video calls with their friends.

I was terrified when I was pregnant that I would be an awful mother. I knew nothing about how to bring up kids; I only knew what not to do. When Daisy was a baby, I read every book I could get my hands on about bringing up children, but they all contradicted each another. Should I be regimented about how I carried out sleep training, forcing her into a strict schedule, or take a more relaxed approach and meet her needs as they arise? Both approaches could not be taken at the same time.

One book told me that if my toddler has a tantrum about something, then give them what they want. I tried this in the supermarket. "I want a biscuit," screamed Daisy. I headed to the biscuit aisle and picked up a packet of chocolate biscuits. "Not a chocolate biscuit! Iced biscuit!" I opened up a packet of iced biscuits, and offered her one. "Not pink biscuit! Hate pink! No! No! No!" She knocked it out of my hand so that it flew out and hit an elderly man walking past. He was not happy and my saying "sorry" did nothing to help. Next thing, Daisy prostrated herself and started screaming and pummelling the floor with her fists.

I walked away and left her there. Not for long, though, as I was soon gripped with a fear that she would be abducted. When I went rushing back, she was still prostrate on the floor, screaming. Thank goodness. Not the type of child that would appeal to a kidnapper. I wiped the snot from her face with one of the many tissues I always have about my person and waited for the storm to pass. It took three more minutes – I timed it. From then on, I always liked to time the length of Daisy's tantrums; timing things is one of my more successful coping strategies. It may seem like tantrums of toddlers last forever, but it was rare for one of Daisy's to go beyond five minutes. As for George, his were usually over within two.

Despite my haphazard mothering, I have somehow ended up living in this pleasant home with what appear to be socially adept children.

I try to keep everything under control, such as by keeping the house tidy, which is challenging when you live with three messy people. One tactic for distracting myself

Chapter Three

from any underlying unease is to fantasise about different ways of disposing of Dad. Let me count the ways ...

I remind myself that this is a good time for me. The weather is great, and I don't have to see anyone. Also, I enjoy the routine, where each day is almost the same as the day before. I can still do my work, as my job has always meant working from home. Some accountants may tell you that there is a lot more to the profession than just adding up numbers, that it is creative in its own way. I'm not looking for excitement, though; there is a peace that comes from doing calculations, moving numbers around and working with spreadsheets. Spreadsheets make sense; they don't mess with you like people do.

I get enough excitement from walking Jeff the Dog to Richmond Park. I always make sure I do at least ten thousand steps, which I measure on the smartwatch Henry bought for me last Christmas. It counts all sorts of things, and I like how it takes my pulse at regular intervals. Although it is of some concern that my resting pulse is often over eighty-five beats per minute.

Today, my walking pulse averages a hundred beats per minute, which is more acceptable. You're meant to always have your dog on a lead in the park, but I decide that I have found a spot where he can safely wander about, so I let him off.

Jeff is the absolute love of Henry's life. I used to be, but I do not have a cute, furry face (though as I get older, I have noticed some nasty stray hairs starting to sprout from on my chin). When the kids came along, Henry could engulf them with all his love, but once they grew up, it was inevitable that we would get a dog to meet Henry's need to look after something.

So we searched online for a rescue dog and that is

where Henry saw the one for him. Now, Jeff the Dog is not the best looking – he is a mix of a greyhound and miniature schnauzer. He has a terrier-like square head, horrible scruffy fur, and this strange skinny body with that concave stomach that greyhounds have. Despite his weird appearance, or maybe because of it, Henry adores him.

One of the problems with Henry is that he tends to love kids and animals to a fault. In other words, he spoils them. Jeff the Dog is definitely spoilt. I should not let Jeff the Dog off the lead in the park, I know I shouldn't, but I also know that Henry likes Jeff to have freedom. Plus, it is so warm and sunny and there is no one around. I know I am taking a calculated risk, as my risks are always carefully calculated, but I reckon there is little chance of anything untoward happening. I soon find I have left out a key factor.

Although there are no other people near us, I fail to spot the large stag. Deer don't like dogs at the best of times, and Jeff the Dog is not one to leave them in peace. He sees the stag, and that is it – he is off. The stag, instead of running away, decides to fight. Next thing I know, Jeff the Dog is tearing towards me, followed by this huge beast, and I start screaming. With good reason, if you google deaths by wild animals, you will discover that deer are about as dangerous as they come.

Jeff the Dog is a speedy little monster, so he disappears whilst the stag gets closer and closer and then rears up on its hind legs. I instinctively crouch as time slows and I wait for hooves to crash down on me. Blood pounds in my head. So this is how it ends. What a humiliating death. I am bound to be in the local papers.

Before I find out if your life does flash before your eyes before you die, I'm granted a reprieve. I hear the hooves

Chapter Three

landing heavily on the ground close to me, and then the stag snorts and runs off – back to chasing Jeff the Dog I imagine.

I stay down on the ground for what I estimate to be four minutes before I compose myself and head back to the path. I am too scared to call for Jeff the Dog, in case he is still being chased. So I find a bench and just sit there, trembling and feeling sick. My pulse is a hundred and forty beats per minute.

Six minutes later, Jeff the Dog appears, looking pleased with himself. He spots me and immediately puts his front legs on my lap wagging his tail madly. One good thing about pets is that they love you no matter how bad you are. They also don't give a damn about what is happening in the news.

As with any event that could have ended badly, I try to think of a way that such a situation could end badly for Dad. Could I get a deer to attack him? But it helps to have a dog with you to attract deer and Dad hates Jeff the Dog.

Dad is super fit, and I have walked with him around Richmond Park many times. He always takes the lead, mocking me for how slow I am. "You struggling there, knucklehead? You've always been a slow one.

"Remember your school sports day when you were ten? How your mother and I laughed when we saw you way, way behind all the other kids, running around the school field. Even though you were one of the oldest and biggest! Maybe that's your problem – carrying all those extra pounds doesn't just make you look like a sack of potatoes; it slows you down, too."

Dad has never liked overweight people, and used to insist my mother put me on diets throughout my childhood. The first one was just after that fateful sports day. My dad shouted at me in the car about how I had been a complete embarrassment and that other parents must have been wondering if I could really have been his child ... How could such a father, in such great shape, have such a useless lump as a daughter?

The first diet was miserable. All the diets were. I loved my food, but a diet meant food that I did not love. No sweets, no cakes, no biscuits. Plenty of grapefruit, with no sugar on top to counter its bitterness. I learnt the calories of every food off by heart from a little book that Dad gave me, and even to this day I still know roughly how many calories I have eaten every day. Though the figures are based on that book I had as a kid, so they are probably out of date now. But I don't want to update them; I don't want to get too obsessed.

There were charts on the bathroom walls of all our weights. By the time I was sixteen, my weight was allowed to go up to eight stone, same as my mother's. My dad's weight never went above twelve stone, and never below eleven stone, twelve pounds. He could control his weight because he had self-discipline, he constantly told us. And luckily for us, he had enough discipline to control our weight, too.

When I asked Mum why she let him dictate to us how much we weighed, she said I should be grateful for it. "As the saying goes," she'd tell me, "You can't be too rich or too thin."

Dad judged us both on our appearances, and didn't care about any other achievements or attributes. When I would bring my school reports home, he wouldn't even cast an eye over my results. He would throw them straight in the bin. "Being clever at school gets you nowhere. You need to look good, then hope some stupid bastard will marry you. Just make sure he is a rich bastard, like me."

I knew one thing. I never wanted to marry anyone who

Chapter Three

was remotely like my dad. Which I didn't. Henry noticed my careful monitoring of my weight early on in our relationship and was concerned about me. He said that I should just eat what I fancy, when I am hungry, and stop worrying about my weight. Especially as I was on the skinny side, which he claimed I was, though I never felt skinny. I have always been able to grab handfuls of flesh around my middle. Henry always said that if I didn't have a bit of padding, it would be worrying.

I tried to stop worrying about calories and weight, and to some extent I succeeded. I threw away my scales for a start. In the back of my mind, though, I always have a calorie calculator totting up the day's food, and when I put on my clothes in the morning, I can't help worrying each day that they are feeling a bit tighter. So far, I have never had to go up a dress size, so it must all be in my head.

Dad dismissed Henry the minute he met him. The first time Henry met my parents was a warm evening in a tapas restaurant in Richmond.

I had warned Henry that my parents would probably be rude and the meal would not be a pleasant one, but Henry said that it had to happen. That he had to meet them sometime. We had been going out for a year by then, and had just started our first jobs. Mine was as a trainee graduate accountant in a second-rate accountancy firm (second-rate according to Dad) and Henry was a junior sub-editor at a car magazine.

When we walked into the restaurant, my parents were already sitting at the table. They barely glanced up when we arrived. My dad's first words were: "You're late."

"Only by five minutes – we had transport problems." The truth was that Henry had held me up – he was a terrible timekeeper, still is. "Mum, Dad, this is Henry, whom I've been telling you about."

"I thought you said his name was Dave?" Mum said. Dave was the name of my first boyfriend who had dumped me just before I went to uni, but by this time, Mum's brain was in a permanent fog due to the amount of Valium she was taking.

Henry laughed. "So who is this Dave then? Should I be worried, Laura?"

Before I could say anything, Dad said, "All Laura's boyfriends are a terrible waste of space, but that doesn't mean you shouldn't be worried. Depends whether you're an even greater waste of space! So what do you do?"

Henry explained he was a sub-editor, but Dad's eyes glazed over almost as soon as Henry spoke. He cut across him to say, "Hurry up, everyone, and decide what you're eating. Looks like you should be thinking along the lines of a salad, Laura. With no dessert."

Henry and I stayed silent throughout the rest of the meal, whilst my dad told the same old stories of the incredible deals he had put together during his trading days. All his stories were about making money. Dad also liked to tell stories about all the women he had slept with, but he usually (although not always) told these when Mum was out of earshot. Luckily, that evening, he decided to stick to stories that didn't involve sex, as these always made me feel sick.

When we were not responding with enough enthusiasm to one of his stories. Dad shouted, "I think you're not listening to me, Laura, am I boring you?"

By this time, he had decided that Henry was not worth considering, and he never considered my mum to be worthy of much attention.

Chapter Three

"No, Dad, that's a great story; it is just that I have heard it before."

"Okay then, if you know it so well, perhaps you could finish it then. How much money did I make?"

"An impressive amount."

"Yes, it was very impressive. If you had been listening, you would know exactly how impressive. I have to repeat these stories because you don't pay attention to the details. You certainly never get the lesson from them. The lesson that you have singularly failed to absorb is that you have to love money to make money. You spend your time adding up figures, knucklehead, but you don't get the point. Being a slave to clients and companies is for fools. But then making money has never been your strong suit, and neither has making the most of your looks."

He laughed and laughed, slapping his hand down on the table. I noticed the two women at the next table threw Dad looks of annoyance, which Dad saw, too. He got up and went over to them. "If you don't like other people in restaurants enjoying themselves, then perhaps you should stay in." When he returned to our table, he sat down triumphantly. If the women had been younger and more to Dad's taste, he would never have been so rude; he would have been flirty and slimy instead, which is even worse in my opinion. The women he had just shouted at got up and moved to another table.

Henry was horribly embarrassed and, after the meal, complained that both my parents had completely ignored him. "You got off lightly then," I laughed. "Being ignored by them is so much better than when they notice you and decide you need improving."

After that, Henry understood when I complained about my dad. Before meeting my parents, he had always been rather mystified about why I seemed to care so little for them. In the same way I had been confused by his obvious adoration of his own parents, especially his mum.

He used to actually want to call her up on the phone every day, and he would willingly spend up to an hour talking to her, laughing away. When I got to meet his parents, which was soon after he had the nasty experience of meeting mine, it all fell into place. Henry's mum and dad were genuinely nice people. As was his sister, Polly. I realised Henry belonged to one of those peculiar, happy families with loving, nurturing parents. You don't come across them very often. It is a tragedy how it all ended. I don't think Henry has ever recovered.

Chapter Four

Fourth sign of a psychopath: enjoyment of pain and suffering

Henry

I have two mouth ulcers. My knees are playing up and in the mornings I can hardly bend down at all. Just feeding Jeff can send agonising pains shooting up my legs. As for my mind, well ...

Having this time stuck indoors could have been ideal, if only things were different. I am trying to make the best of it. I write every day. I'm spending more time with my family and finally getting round to those jobs I've been meaning to do for years. The windows and doors are all freshly painted. I'm going for cycle rides, cooking meals from scratch, tackling the garden.

I'm doing everything right on the outside. And the family sees the same, old Henry they have always known. What they don't know is that I am not their Henry anymore. I am someone else doing an impression of him.

Once we are allowed out, I have to make sure that I can move forward, and away.

I don't want Laura or the kids to be worse off, or to lose this house. The only way I can afford to walk away is if Laura gets her inheritance. Which she bloody deserves after all that monster has put her through. Put us all through. He should be in prison by rights.

I still can't forgive myself for not acting immediately after what he did to Daisy, but it was hard to know exactly how to respond at the time. Killing Brian now seems to be a cop out in some ways, as it serves my ends so well. The right thing to do would be to report Brian, to get the police involved, to excavate all his crimes and misdemeanours so that he is humiliated in public.

That would be the right thing to do. But it is easier to kill him.

Chapter Five

Fifth sign of a psychopath: belief that you are special

Laura

By week four of lockdown, the total number of UK recorded COVID deaths is over twenty-two thousand. As well as the news, my workload is beginning to weigh heavily. Apart from the end-of-year accounts I need to finish, one of my clients has furloughed his employees and is worried about his company going under. Dave Chapman is the publisher of an online magazine, which relied on events for its income, so suddenly his main source of money has disappeared, although he is trying to get online events off the ground. He is always calling me up asking about the latest government grants and schemes, and as all the legislation is so new it is hard for me to keep on top of things.

Dave Chapman also happens to be the boyfriend who broke my heart before I met Henry. When Dave got in touch with me on Facebook years ago, Henry told me he must only be after one thing. And Henry was right in a way – Dave was after one thing. An accountant.

We have met up many times over the years I have been working for him, and there is no remnant spark of attraction, despite Henry's implying that there must be. We are both happily married now.

I do worry, however, that I am beginning to get on Henry and the kids' nerves. I think I am being cheery, considering the circumstances, but whenever I ask anyone to help with the housework or give me some peace and quiet whilst I work, I get accused of being a nag.

"Mum, you need to count your blessings," says Daisy after I ask her if maybe she could do her yoga exercises in another room, rather than the lounge where I am working. She is in a downward dog at the time, and stays in that position rather than packing up her mat.

As much as I like the monotony of my work, the new demands of Dave are rather onerous. And does he have to keep ringing me up all the time? It is much more efficient to put everything down in emails, but Dave says he likes to pick up the phone and actually speak to people: "I'm an old-school type of guy."

I find that as I get older, I can't handle all this extra work very well. In fact, I realise, I don't like working half as much as I used to. I would rather like to retire now. I could spend more time with Henry. We could maybe go travelling together, with Jeff the Dog, when we are allowed out of the prison of Richmond, as lovely as it is.

Naturally, this train of thought takes me back to my regular daydream of killing Dad. He lives in that great big house, all on his own, and as much as he is always threatening to cut me out of his will, so far he hasn't and I am the

Chapter Five

main beneficiary. I know his will inside out as writing it, and rewriting it, is a major preoccupation of his.

* * *

When I visit Dad's crumbling country pile in the heartlands of the Surrey Hills, he often likes to drag me up to his study to show me his papers. His study walls are covered with portraits of him. He has commissioned oil paintings to mark significant birthdays, when he was thirty, forty, fifty, sixty, and seventy.

Each one is in a slightly different style, but none are as fantastic as Dad thinks, but then they are limited by the subject matter (in my opinion, that is – Dad thinks there is no greater object of interest than his own fine physique). Thank goodness the artist persuaded Dad to put more clothes on than in the last portrait. Dad's idea had been to be in a posing pouch, kind of like Mr Universe.

Dad's personal trainer at the time was always flattering Dad about his musculature which, has to be said, is incredible for his age. Although, judging from the photos Dad used to send me of him working out in skimpy shorts, even a well-toned seventy-year-old man is no Adonis. The pics of my dad posing in his shorts were a sight to behold. And for some reason he also posted these photos to my kids who were still at infant school at the time. He couldn't see why this wouldn't be a thrill for them. Needless to say, it certainly had an impact.

So we sit by Dad's desk, whilst Dad pulls out the various files and ledgers he wants me to look at. All the while, I feel the five pairs of eyes from Dad's portraits boring into me. Dad likes to show me his share portfolio so I can congratulate him on his many wise choices. I know better than to mention his unwise choices, of which there are quite a few – a large number of Woolworths shares have been a spectacular disaster for example.

"You remember where my will is?" Dad usually asks. "Just in case anything happens?"

"Yes, Dad."

It is in one of the top drawers of his desk – the drawer he keeps unlocked. There is another drawer that is always locked. When I ask Dad what's in that one, he says a man has to have some privacy.

"But where is the key, Dad," I say. "I will need to open it if you're no longer around?"

"Don't you worry about that now. I don't plan on going anywhere soon."

I don't like to point out that the whole reason for him dragging me up to his study (again) was to go through what to do following his death. I just let Dad do his usual speech on how I am the sole beneficiary of his estate. He likes to keep the subject interesting by sometimes making out that I don't deserve to inherit anything and saying he is thinking of leaving everything to charity. *"I think you have more than enough money – your kids seem spoilt rotten. Do you think the National Trust might like to take over this place, and turn it into a museum?"*

I know better than to ever disagree about any of Dad's opinions, so I always nod along to whatever he suggests.

He also likes to remind me that it is up to me to make sure his sister, Auntie Penny, gets the best painting in his study. The best painting in his opinion because it was executed by him.

When Dad was a teenager, he did a watercolour picture of Auntie Penny in his school art class, based on a photograph of her as a baby. The painting is sweet, not bad for

Chapter Five

something done by a fifteen-year-old. His parents had it framed, and the picture now hangs in Dad's study, just above his desk, below his favourite portrait of himself.

My aunt has no idea that I am (currently) the sole beneficiary of Dad's will apart from this watercolour. Over the years, Auntie Penny has spent far more time than she should have visiting my dad and generally being a good sister to him. I think she does this because she is a kind person; I find it hard to believe she actually likes him. Dad has always hinted, or rather lied, that she and her family would be well looked after when he dies.

Auntie Penny must know there is no real good in Dad. After all, she has known him longer than I have. There are many stories of the awful things he has done to her, starting with him trying to kill her when she was a baby by putting her in the oven. He was stopped by their mum, just in time. He wasn't going to cook his sister, just suffocate her with gas. An idea he had got from his mum, as a few times he had come home from school to find her crouched in the kitchen with her head in the oven. She never put the gas on, so always survived these suicide attempts. No, Dad didn't have a great childhood either.

And neither did Auntie Penny. She would be devastated to find out that all she is going to get after years of putting up with her brother is that childish watercolour.

Whenever I go to Dad's house, I am overwhelmed by the huge amount of stuff he has. Stuff I know I will have to sort out when he is gone. On balance, I always decide, sorting out his mountain of possessions and papers is still preferable to having to spend much more time with him.

Before this pandemic, my main fantasies of killing Dad usually focused on a spontaneous act. Pushing him off a cliff, for example.

The pushing-him-off-a-cliff idea was top of my mind when I went on a weekend away with him to Penzance. The summer after Mum's death, Dad said he wanted to go away on holiday, and couldn't face going on his own, so I suggested a trip to Cornwall. Dad said that it was only fair that I pay for the holiday, as he had had to fork out on our family holidays when I was a kid. I knew he was expecting me to whisk him off on a five-star cruise in the Caribbean, but I thought he was lucky I was taking him anywhere.

We went on a sleeper train to Penzance and then arrived at a cute (in my opinion) B&B. "Your business is obviously doing badly" was all Dad had to say about it. On the first morning at breakfast, there was another couple in the dining room. They must have recently got together, I thought, as they were holding hands over the table. Which I hoped Dad hadn't spotted, as two men holding hands was bound to send him into a rage. Dad didn't spot the hand-holding, but then they pulled their hands apart as Dad approached them. Dad decided to ruin the start of their day by boring and annoying them in equal measure.

At first, one of the men – and, to a lesser extent, his partner – looked pleased to be engaging in conversation. My dad said a friendly hello and then asked them where they were from. So far, so good. And when the response was "Canada", Dad's monologue began and their smiles froze.

"Canada?" Dad asked. "Oh, I've never been to Canada, but I've heard all about it." He then listed all the great Canadian lakes and all the places he had been in America – because that was as close as he had been to exploring Canada – and then he finished by saying all the opinions he had about Canadians. For example, *Canadian people are very dull*. "I am sure you aren't dull though!."

The younger-looking of the two said: "Yes, we are just

as dull as everyone else in Canada, which is why we like to have a quiet breakfast. It was nice meeting you, though. Hope you have a great break here in Penzance."

Dad came and joined me at our table, *harrumphing* as he sat down. He whispered very loudly, "Not the friendliest, the Canadians", before discussing whether he should have a full English because it was full of protein, or more of a "runner's breakfast" so he would feel lighter as we set off on the long walk we had planned. "You should just have fruit," he said to me. "You've got enough fat on you to power you through the day. What am I saying ... It could power you through a whole year!" As to be expected after one of his brilliant jokes, he slapped his hand down hard on the table and brayed out a few loud laughs. Behind him, I could see both men throw him looks of disgust. I shared their pain.

Really, it was for the good of everyone who came across my dad if I could dispose of him as quickly as possible, I thought for the umpteenth time as we marched along the coastal path. Just one shove and it would all be over.

As much as my arm ached to push my dad, though, I knew it would take more than one shove to get him off the coastal path and then over the edge. And he wouldn't go without a fight, that was for sure. A fight that I would lose. If a body was going to be flung from the top off the cliff, it would be mine. So murder plan number twenty seven (a rough estimate) was put to bed.

The plan that I eventually settled on did take seed on that trip, though. On our way back to the B&B we went past many blackberry bushes, and occasionally Dad would stop, pick a few, and stuff them in his mouth. "You can't beat free food," he said.

Dad does love a bargain, and more than that, he likes to get something for nothing. I was once with him in a supermarket and he got very excited about a sign for free-range eggs. "Free eggs?" he said. "I like the sound of those!"

Blackberry picking is a yearly event for me, not because I want to save money, but more for the pleasure of the mindfulness of the picking, and another excuse to spend time walking along Isle of Wight country lanes. Plus, Henry likes to make batches of blackberry jam.

We have a small, two-bedroom cottage in the village of Bembridge in the Isle of Wight that Henry and his sister, Polly, inherited eight years ago when their uncle passed away. It is our favourite holiday place, and we always spend as much of the summer there as we can. It's five minutes away from a beach and the coastal path.

I also take my friend Charlotte there for weekends away, and it was on a weekend away with her in the autumn of 2019 that my murder plan developed further. Charlotte has known me since I was eleven. We became friends on the first day of secondary school. I think Charlotte saved my life – I'm sure I had a sign saying "Bully Me" over my head, but Charlotte ignored that sign and for some bizarre reason stuck to my side for the whole grim five years we were there.

And she has stuck with me ever since. It is even thanks to her that I am with Henry now. She found him first. She was really generous when I got together with Henry – she says I didn't steal him from her, as her relationship with him was already over anyway. Henry and I used to feel bad about it at the beginning, but Charlotte always seemed genuinely happy for us. And we both felt much better about everything once she got together with Martin soon after.

"You're not taking this one off me too!" she used to say in the early days. As if Martin would ever look at anyone else – I have never met a couple more perfect for each other. I sometimes envy how comfortable they look in each other's

Chapter Five

company and how they laugh so uproariously at each other's jokes. Perhaps I should laugh harder at Henry's. Usually, when he makes "witty asides", the kids and I roll our eyes and accuse him of making awful Dad jokes. I am sure he used to be wittier, before we had the children. Or maybe I just laughed more easily when I was younger.

Charlotte is easy to make laugh, because when we are all together she often gets quite overcome with hysteria following one of Henry's anecdotes. She also sometimes gets the giggles when she is alone with me, but I worry that she is laughing more *at* me than *with* me.

Charlotte is now a landscape gardener. Passionate about the outdoors, she is always pestering me to take her to our place by the sea, so I often do. As well as liking long walks and nature, just after we first got the cottage, Charlotte enjoyed escaping her two boys, who are the same age as my kids. As great as they are now, Charlotte's boys were exhausting when they were younger. Unlike my two, who have always been happy slumped in front of a screen, her two have never been able to sit still for long. Not that surprising, as Charlotte is always full of beans and Martin was once a professional rugby player and is now a trainer. "Sporty" is one word for that household; "loud" and "messy" also fit. When you get inside her front door, you have to negotiate a hallway floor covered with trainers, wellingtons, hockey sticks, rugby balls and unpleasant-smelling sports kit. It is an obstacle course worthy of an army training ground. It would drive me mad living like that. Well, madder ... I am not exactly completely sane after all.

By the autumn of 2019, Charlotte's boys, like my two, were away at uni, and Charlotte was bereft, missing them so much. Most of the drive to Portsmouth Harbour, she was dabbing her eyes with a handkerchief and wondering if Alex (her youngest) was truly happy in Bournemouth or was just putting on a brave face. *I wish you would put on a braver face*, I thought but didn't say it.

I missed Daisy and George, too – or rather, I thought I did. Sometimes I am not sure if I really feel the emotions, or am simply recognising what the right emotions should be. Either way, I did get where Charlotte was coming from, even if her constant sniffling was grating. I silently counted down from a hundred, taking seven away each time, to prevent me from saying anything, from giving away my true, unkind nature.

That weekend we spent part of our walks gathering "produce". As well as blackberries, Charlotte was excited by all the mushrooms. On one trip along the stunning coast from Bembridge to Sandown, where the view from the top of the cliffs is enough to make you believe there is a God, I stood and counted the number of shipping containers I could see in the distance waiting to go into port (nine). Charlotte's eyes were cast downwards as she spotted different mushroom varieties and explained what they all were to me.

"We have to have some of these for breakfast," she said, indicating some perfectly ordinary-looking mushrooms.

"You sure you know what you're doing? Positive those are the safe ones?" I said.

Charlotte bent down and, picking one, turned it over: "These are just field mushrooms. See these gills? You have to avoid mushrooms with white gills. These are fine. Anyway, the really poisonous death cap mushrooms are nothing like this ..."

The next morning Charlotte was very excited about cooking the mushrooms, and the sound of frying accompa-

Chapter Five

nied her singing, a bad rendition of the song "Lovely Day". Charlotte loves to sing. Sometimes I think Henry should have stuck with her, as he is always singing too. If he were still with her, the home they could have made together would be constantly full of the sound of singing and laughter. I never inflict my singing voice on anyone; it wouldn't be fair. I don't even like to talk in the mornings, but Charlotte knows this about me and never tries to engage me in conversation until after the first coffee.

The morning of the mushroom-cooking, I was pouring out my first coffee when Charlotte exclaimed: "Damn! I'll have to throw this batch away. I seem to have picked a Yellow Stainer by mistake – thank God it goes yellow or I would never have known."

I was put off the idea of eating mushrooms for breakfast by now, but as I was my usual mute self, Charlotte placed another batch of mushrooms in the pan, and apparently these were fine. As she presented them to me on buttered toast, I felt it would be churlish to refuse them, so I looked as excited as I was able, which was probably not very excited. I thought they were no more delicious than supermarket mushrooms, but I kept quiet, whilst Charlotte explained that the mushroom that had turned yellow was not terribly poisonous but would have given us stomach troubles.

The breakfast had no long-lasting physical effects at all. It did have long-term effects in other ways though, as it was those mushrooms that inspired the final plan.

Chapter Six

Sixth sign of a psychopath: need for excessive admiration

Laura

The total number of UK COVID-related deaths is now thirty-two thousand. It is week six of lockdown, and the novelty of isolation is definitely wearing off. Every time I pass by someone I know on the Richmond to Twickenham riverside path, I am surprised at how pleased I am to see them and how much I want to stop and have a chat. At a safe distance, naturally.

One thing I have noticed is that two metres, which is an easy distance to understand, means completely different things to so many people. I see some people backing away in horror as anyone comes close to twenty feet towards them, whilst joggers (especially the older, male ones) think that two metres is about six inches and you can almost feel their breath upon your neck as they lumber up behind you.

I feel safe outside, not just because I assume I have anti-

Chapter Six

bodies now. I am sure you would have to get close to someone to catch the virus in the outdoors, yet I find myself feeling disproportionately angry if anyone fails to respect my personal space. I also notice, as I watch films on TV, how strange it seems to see people hugging each other, people they hardly know! I wonder if I will ever feel comfortable about kissing a stranger on the cheek again (not that I ever particularly felt comfortable doing that)?

We all like to take Jeff the Dog out for a walk these days, and I worry that the dog, who before always loved going for walks and used to jump up and down when you showed him his lead, is now showing less enthusiasm when we take the lead off its hook. My slot for walking him is usually after I finish work, around four or five pm. My most common route is along a path I like to follow that skirts the edge of the park at its highest points, as this offers the most spectacular views of a canopy of luscious trees, which grow more verdant by the day. It also is a route that means I get all my steps done.

This afternoon, however, I decide to walk along the river towards Twickenham. This is a longer walk, and I should notch up twenty thousand steps by the time I get home – which is just as well as by my (probably inaccurate) calorie-counting, I consumed nearly two thousand seven hundred calories yesterday. A couple of extra glasses of red wine pushed me over my average daily calorie intake.

I am delighted today to see Charlotte and her dog, Scratchy (old labradoodle), coming towards me just as I walk past the manmade houseboat of one of Twickenham's local characters. The home consists of two rafts tied together, one raft supporting a large man-made construction of a hut made out of rubbish lashed together with string, and the other is his homemade floating garden. Henry is always going on about living on a houseboat, whilst I always shudder when I pass this, imagining how uncomfortable it must be to live on the Thames.

I know before I hear my name being bellowed out at a hundred decibels that it is going to happen, and flinch in advance. Charlotte is loud. As she is always telling me: *"It is funny how you hate to be embarrassed so much in public, Laura, and then you go and choose about the most embarrassing friend you could possibly have."* It is true that Charlotte is an embarrassing person to be around. Everyone always notices her because of her loud voice and the often horribly personal things she is bellowing about, but it is not true that I chose her as a friend. I have never been in a position to choose friends; they (and I am talking about a total of about three here) have always chosen me. Beggars, as the expression goes, cannot be choosers. As awkward as Charlotte often makes me feel in public, I will always be inordinately grateful that she has picked me to be her friend.

Soon we are facing each other, the required two metres apart, whilst Jeff the Dog and Scratchy fail to respect any social distancing whatsoever and do their usual mutual bottom-sniffing.

Charlotte looks bright and happy, and admits that lockdown is going well for her. "I feel guilty as so many people are suffering, and having to work in such hard jobs, whilst for me it is a bit like a holiday. Plus, I so love having Alex and Tom home, although it is also nice to get out from a house full of three big men ... So how are you? And tell me, how is your dad?"

Charlotte has always enjoyed hearing stories about the latest bad behaviour from my dad.

Chapter Six

"He's decided it is time to get that book published. The one about him and his amazing life."

"He's written an autobiography?"

"No, of course not. He is really angry because he approached some of the top ghostwriters by email and phone, thinking they would be at a loose end and desperate to write about him, but none of them were at all interested."

"Quelle surprise ..."

"Then he offers it to writers who usually charge to write biographies, but says he won't pay them, seeing that they could make a lot of money from the book, as his life has been so eventful, plus he is a great man – surely they must have heard of him? This is after sending them that one newspaper article that appeared in *The Times* in his heyday, which is now forty years ago. "

"No takers, I assume?"

"Of course there were no takers! But guess what, the worst is yet to come! He then calls me up and says that he would be willing to give Henry the opportunity to write the book."

"Lucky Henry!"

"I know. He said that, although Henry is not the best writer, it is only fair to give him the chance to make some money out of proper project. He said that he was willing to let Henry take ten per cent of the profits!"

"What profits?"

"Precisely! You would have to pay booksellers a lot of money to have a book with my dad's face on the cover. Henry was not amused."

"Typical of your dad. So how did you tell him that Henry has refused?"

"I haven't yet. I can't face the terrible shouting and accusations of ingratitude that will ensue. I have just said that Henry is working on a novel, and that we will get back to him after that."

We say goodbye, partly because we are getting so many disapproving looks from people, as some have to deviate from their straight walking and running routes to stay two metres away from us. There is plenty of room at this part of the Thames path, but there is also plenty of path rage, with people becoming enraged at what they believe to be the thoughtlessness of others. They are probably missing getting angry in their cars, as this is the usual place for travel rage, and so their pent-up feelings are being channelled into their daily walks.

Talking of road rage, this is something that Henry – who is fairly even tempered usually – suffers from in spades. He must save up all of his frustration for when he is driving. Should we have to stop at a red light ever – which, let's face it, is inevitable – he lets forth a string of expletives. Apparently, there would never be any need to stop at a red light if the "twat" in the car ahead of us hadn't been so slow...

As Henry is now not able to expel his anger in his usual fashion in the car, I notice that he is getting grumpier. The DIY he has started doing in the house is accompanied by a soundtrack of Radio 1, but as well as Henry's habitual singing along, I also hear him swearing a lot at the idiotic things the DJs are saying.

We have never been a couple who argues much, we tend to hold the same views on most things, or I assume we do. Henry is particularly in agreement with me that my dad is a nightmare.

I should have taken Henry's advice years ago to cut my Dad out of my life. When he used to suggest it when the kids were little, I'd argue that it would not be fair on Daisy

Chapter Six

and George, as my dad's money was their only hope of getting any decent inheritance. Henry always used to reply that it just wasn't worth it. Then I would say that, even if I did cut him out, what about my mum? It was just too difficult. Now I argue that I can't abandon Dad, saying that one can't just abandon an eighty-five-year-old living on their own.

Looking back, it would have been better to have erased my dad from my life when he was younger, as it would ultimately be kinder to us all than my current plans to get rid of him through murder.

Although my murderous plans, I tell myself, are something I will surely never carry out. I know I tried to infect him with COVID-19, but that was just a stupid spur-of-the-moment idea, and luckily it didn't work, or I would be in pieces. This is what I tell myself. Who knows if any of us actually had the virus anyway? None of us were tested.

When I get back home from my walk with Jeff the Dog, (twenty thousand-step target achieved), I can smell that dinner is cooking, which is great as I am starved. Well, not really, but I am certainly feeling peckish. Am I eating more over lockdown?, I worry to myself as I sit down to a pad Thai, cooked as a joint effort by Daisy and George.

During dinner, I get a phone call. Glancing at the screen, I see it's Dad. "Don't answer it!" says Henry, so I don't, but I call Dad straight back as soon as I leave the table.

He tells me that he is running low on wine, and to add a few more bottles to the shop I am doing for him tomorrow. He has been unable to master online shopping and he likes to see me, so that he gets to see "some bloody person" during this lonely period.

As it happens, Dad sees quite a few people. He has

succeeded in getting a gang of fools running around after him, and this is giving him immense pleasure. His Polish gardener Jakub still comes and he has even succeeded in getting his cleaner to agree to come every week. Teresa, who has been cleaning his house for at least twenty years – and who was one of my mum's favourite people in the whole world – is a saint, and she should have refused. Teresa did say, at first, when Dad asked her to clean his house during this lockdown, that it would not be fair on either his or her own family if she were to do the cleaning. Dad was having none of it. "I told her not to be so bloody ridiculous. This house is big enough for us to keep well over two yards apart, and anyway, it's good to keep busy at her age."

As well as Jakub, Teresa and me going over to Dad's house every week, he also has neighbours dropping in, as he finds he has run out of basic necessities nearly every day and calls them up asking if they can pop out and get them. There is no way he can possibly have run out of necessities, as I know from doing his shopping that he has stockpiled everything you can possibly think of. There is enough food in that house to feed a family of four for months. If not years.

At the end of the call, Dad says: "Maybe you could get Daisy to help carry the shopping. As the weather is so nice, I expect she isn't wearing much right now, and it does an old man good to see a pretty girl's legs!"

"Dad, that's not appropriate," I say.

I hate him so much, but you know that.

"For God's sake, Laura, stop being such a prude. Why does Daisy flaunt her body all the time if she doesn't want people to look at it?"

Of course I have no intention of taking Daisy with me

Chapter Six

to be ogled by her grandfather. Not after what happened at Christmas. And before.

I wish I could cut out of my brain all the things I know about my dad's attitude towards women and sex. I wish I could unhear all the unpleasant things he has told me, or I have overheard. When the truth came out about Jimmy Savile and public opinion turning so violently against him, Dad was shocked. Not by what Savile had done, but the public condemnation of it.

He said: "It makes me question some of the things I have done."

I was amazed that Dad might actually feel he had done something wrong, and replied: "If you feel uncomfortable about anything, perhaps you could try and make amends?"

"I don't feel that bad!" Dad shouted back.

These days I try and avoid any conversations about anything apart from the mundane, such as the weekly shopping list. Dad prefers me to get his food from different shops, including Aldi and Lidl, so that I can get the best bargains for him, but it is so much more pleasant to go to the local Waitrose, so I do.

After the most recent shop, as I unpack the bags in Dad's kitchen (he claims to have a bad back and be unable to carry it into the house himself, despite the many hours he spends in his gym each day), I hear the usual sighs of disapproval.

"You know you could have saved at least £20 if you had shopped more carefully. I don't think it is fair that I should have to pay for your laziness, so I am sure you won't mind if I knock £20 off the payment I send you. I expect other daughters are doing the shopping for their elderly fathers and not asking for any payment for it at all ..."

The difference is that other daughters don't have such rich, nasty men as their fathers, I think.

"As you are here," says Dad. "You may as well come up and we can go through the will ..."

So I trudge up the stairs and go through the regular routine in Dad's study. As soon as we sit down, Dad's mobile starts ringing. He looks at the screen and says: "Ignore the ringing, I'll call them back later."

"Who is it, Dad?"

"Just Geoffrey."

Geoffrey is Dad's solicitor. I have met him many times in my life as he is Dad's oldest and closest friend. They have many things in common, including loving money and being dirty old men. Geoffrey excessively fawned over me when I was young, in a way that made me squirm, although he never did anything outright pervy, apart from always holding my hand too long when we met and pressing his middle finger into my palm for some strange reason.

Dad ignores the ringing phone, but as soon as it stops, it starts up again.

"Christ's sake!" shouts Dad as he looks at the screen.

"Who is it this time?" I ask.

"Never you mind. I don't need another lecture from you. Let me just turn this thing off." Which he does before getting on with telling me yet again about the watercolour that I must give to Auntie Penny. Whilst he goes through the usual routine, I think about how he swindled Penny out of the inheritance he promised her.

When his elderly parents needed help and care, he struck a deal with Penny. He said that if she did all the caring for them, he would waive his share of the inheritance. When they both died, within a year of each other, he forgot all about this deal, and took his full half.

Chapter Six

He tried to make some more money by offering to sell his parents' house at an inflated price to Henry and me. It was sad looking around my grandparents' house, which was empty but so full of childhood memories. It had always been a very shouty house. Dad and his parents never spoke; they only screamed at one another.

"Would you like a cuppa?" Granny would scream at Dad.

"No, I hate your nasty-tasting tea, always stewed for bloody hours!" Dad would shout back.

The house was near a main road, but apart from that, it was just what we were looking for. Henry and I had wanted to move to Richmond, but we couldn't afford the price Dad was selling the house at. We ended up buying a similar house just a few roads away, for £50,000 cheaper. In those days, you could get a doer-upper house in the less popular areas of Richmond for £150,000. That seems crazily cheap now, but it was a struggle for us to pay the mortgage at the time.

Dad never found anyone to buy the house at the price he expected, so he sold it for less than what we paid for our house in the end. He couldn't bear the idea of giving us a good deal, but was willing to sell it to a property developer who ended up making a packet out of it.

As usual after being in Dad's house, I have to take twenty deep, slow breaths in the car so that I can compose myself before the drive home. I wait until my pulse has got down to ninety.

But I still don't feel right, even when I am safely home, sitting in the kitchen pouring my first glass of wine. As soon as Henry sees me, he says: "Do you really need to see your dad so much? You always look like death afterwards. I worry that the stress of seeing him is going to take years off your life. You don't want the prick to be at your funeral instead of the other way around."

"Don't you worry Henry, I am going to make sure that he doesn't outlive me. I promised my mum that I wouldn't let him ruin the rest of my life, and I plan to keep that promise."

Chapter Seven

Seventh sign of a psychopath: ability to make calculated plans

Henry

I am the invisible man. How long have I been living in this house without anyone noticing anything about me?

At first, I assumed that no one was reacting to any change in me because I was doing such a good job of hiding my feelings. Now, I realise, no one sees me. I wonder if they will even notice, let alone care, when I have left? Jeff would be upset, but I am taking him with me. He will be missed more than I will.

Seeing what has happened with Big Paul and Little Paul's marriages has given me some perspective on my own marriage. I met Big Paul at the local pool. Daisy and his son Jack used to have swimming lessons together. I met Little Paul around the same time, in the park by the river, as I pushed Daisy on a swing and he pushed his daughter, Layla, on one next to her. The kids were all so sweet when they were little, not like some of the kids you see around nowadays – they are much more spoilt. Although maybe I am just becoming a grumpy old man ... It goes with the midlife crisis I expect.

Daisy and Layla are still great friends, not quite so sweet now, but still heartbreakingly lovely girls. And break hearts, they do. Sadly, Daisy thinks Little Paul is a complete bastard, as Layla has taken her mum's side. Layla used to adore her dad.

Because both Pauls walked out on their marriages, they are seen as the bad guys, but they are the same men they always were. From what they have said, they'd also begun to feel dispensable in their own homes. They never talk about it in depth, but it is clear that their wives had a part to play in their disenchantment with everything. Both Pauls are happy now with their new partners. They don't slag off their exes; they don't seem bitter about what led them to leave. I think they've actually behaved pretty decently, but I don't dare express that opinion in this house.

I can put forward the Pauls' sides in my book, though. It is sad to see how once-happy families can slowly dissolve, without anyone doing anything particularly wrong.

The only marriage I know that appears to be happy is that of Charlotte and Martin. Not that you ever know what is really happening behind closed doors, of course. Charlotte is like an open book – you don't have to guess what is going on in her head. When we were young and a couple, I found that annoying – her moods changing like the weather, and her spontaneity. "Let's skip lectures today and go to the beach!" she might say. Or she would turn up to a planned date at the cinema to say she just wasn't in the mood for a film after all and drag me out dancing. Why did I not find that charming at the time?

Chapter Seven

Another quality of hers that I found less than charming was her habit of always wanting to know what was going on in my head. She felt it was important to share feelings all the time.

I should have appreciated her more. Martin is a lucky man.

Chapter Eight

Eighth sign of a psychopath: sense of entitlement

Laura

The numbers continue to rise, thirty-six thousand recorded UK COVID-related deaths.

In my daily phone conversation with Dad today, he complains that Daisy and George haven't called him for a while. "You spoke to George a few days ago," I say. I am not going to go into why Daisy hasn't called and will never call again.

"I think most other grandchildren call up their grandparents every day! Not much to ask for a lonely old man to get the occasional call … They will be inheriting all of this one day – the least they can do is make the effort. My friends are always telling me how wonderful their grandkids are, how nothing is too much trouble …"

I zone out for a while, as once Dad gets onto this track (which usually ends with a complaint about how I am also failing him as a daughter), he can go on for some time, and

Chapter Eight

anyway, conversations with Dad are usually one-sided, or rather, his-sided so I can put the phone down on the table until he draws breath.

Since Dad equates love with stuff, it is very important to him that we give him gifts that demonstrate how much we think of him. When George was eight years old, I took him Christmas shopping. He didn't know what to get Grandad, but eventually he selected a keyring that he thought was perfect because it had a corkscrew attachment and he knew Grandad loved his wine.

On Christmas Day, when Dad opened the present from George, he hardly said thank you and spent the whole rest of the day being sneery to George and throwing him nasty looks whenever George said anything.

A few days later, I received a letter from Dad, two pages long, full of bitter words including a paragraph on how he expected a better present from George. The letter went on to list how much he had done for me and the children and how little he got back in return. When he wrote about how much he had done for us, he actually specified the amounts we have cost him over the years, in terms of money he has given us for birthdays and Christmas. Spending money on anyone is extremely painful for Dad.

He feels let down by us, whilst in my heart I feel let down by him. Don't children deserve to be loved by their parents? Even me?

Just before my mum died, she must have pointed this out to him, because I got a call from Dad in another of his rages.

"Your mother hinted that I don't love you! Well, I will have you know that the password I use to open up my computer is 'Laura'!"

"You mean it isn't your own name, Dad – you actually

used *my* name as a password?" I said, knowing that Dad would miss the sarcasm.

"Precisely!" he shouted.

I knew that Dad often liked to change his password as he was paranoid about hackers getting into his emails. I imagined he must have got through plenty before he was down to having to use my name.

Dad himself has been deprived of love. His mum might have said she adored her kids, but her actions spoke otherwise, and his father was away fighting in the war for maybe the key years of Dad's childhood. When his father returned, he expected Dad to help him with the business, and would be waiting for him at the school gates to collect him so that he could work with him on the greengrocer's cart. As well as having to work before school and after school for his father, Dad also had to work weekends. To give my dad his due – he was a hard worker, right until he retired at forty-five. Since then, he has thrown himself into his life of leisure, but rather than working, he works out.

Henry says that my father must also be taking steroids to have bulked up so much, but where would he get hold of those?

Dad has many sad stories of his childhood. When his father was away fighting, these were mainly about his mum and her affairs. He would describe how he would run home when the air raid siren sounded, but his mum wouldn't let him in because she was preoccupied with one of her lovers.

One of these lovers was a Canadian soldier. At my grandad's wake, my grandmother said to my dad, in her usual loud voice so that we could all hear: "It's your fault that I stayed in this country with your old man! I could have gone to Canada and had a life there, but I stayed here because of you!"

Chapter Eight

I was used to hearing Dad and his mum have arguments about all the men she'd had affairs with. I was even quite impressed that she had a couple of flings with residents in the care home where she'd spent her last years.

The children of one of her elderly lovers tried to get Grandma thrown out of the home, accusing her of stealing some of his stuff and making his room stink of her cigarette smoke. They also thought it was Grandma's fault when he ended up dying in bed of a stroke. They thought it must have been brought on by the stress Grandma caused him, not to mention all the sex.

Dad and I would sometimes take his mum on outings away from the home, and one lovely sunny day we were sitting in the tea garden of a National Trust stately home, whilst Dad and Grandma were ruining the peaceful afternoon by screaming at each other. "You could never keep your pants on, you dirty old woman!" shouted Dad. "Even my mate from work, thirty years younger than you! I caught you in bed together!"

And then Grandma decided to revert to her usual topic of her favourite lover that she gave up for Dad and had never got over: "I should have gone to Canada when I had the chance!"

Much to my mortification, everyone in that tea garden fell silent as they listened in horror (or maybe enthralment) as my dad threw accusations at this tiny old woman and she shouted back about how having him had ruined her life.

After my phone call with Dad, I go and look for my yoga mat, so that I can do some relaxation exercises to bring down my heartbeat. I find it in the centre of our bedroom, with Henry sitting on it, cross-legged.

"Henry! So pleased you're trying out yoga."

"I'm not really. I'm just sitting."

"Are you meditating? I'll leave you in peace."

"Yes, thanks, Laura, just give me five minutes."

I shut the bedroom door after I leave and head down to the kitchen to calm myself down there. Is midday too early for a glass of wine? I decide that in this case it isn't, as long as I go for a small one ...

As I sit with my glass of Merlot at the kitchen table, I think about how strange it is that Henry has started meditating. He used to be so chilled that he never needed to take time out, but I suppose these are strange times, and the constant diet of COVID-19 news has been affecting us all. After all, it is not good news – the daily tragedies you hear every day help you to put things into perspective. So many people have lost loved ones.

I must confess, I am often surprised that other people seem so upset that their elderly parent has died. They genuinely love their parents. Is it me who's odd? Or am I right to apportion all the blame onto my dad? Am I scapegoating him? Is he as bad as I think?

Henry soon joins me at the kitchen table and pours himself a glass of wine. I ask him the questions I have just been asking myself.

"You're completely right to put all the blame on your dad. He is the nastiest piece of work I have ever met."

I tell him that I have just come off the phone to Dad and that he wants the kids to call him every day.

"No. No. No. Your father has ruined your life; he is not going to ruin the lives of our kids. I don't want my children having anything to do with him anymore. I told you that after what happened at Christmas. God, it makes me so furious thinking about it. I should have put my hands around his thick old throat and squeezed the life out of him."

Chapter Eight

"But Daisy didn't tell us about it right away. I realised after that it had been a big mistake to have let Dad anywhere near Daisy and George. I should have stopped seeing Dad years ago."

"I've told you that often enough. I might have forgotten about him by now and he'd just be an unpleasant memory, but instead we are in this terrible situation where the only solution is to commit murder. Speaking of which, as the virus failed to kill him, we need to come up with a new plan."

"I have thought of something, but I need to think about the logistics. Anyway, it can't be put into practice until the autumn."

Henry moves his chair closer to mine and puts his arm around me. He speaks softly, as though to comfort me, but there is no comfort in his message. I can't see his expression, but I can feel his pent up rage. "This time I am going to help make sure you go through with it properly. The more I think about what happened at Christmas the more I hate myself for failing to take him on before. But let's face it, he is bigger and stronger than me, so I will have to go with your evil plan, whatever that happens to be ..." Henry removes his arm from my shoulder and picks up his glass again. We are quiet for a moment. I wonder whether we are all talk. It may be our way of coping with my dad, saying we are going to kill him, but deep down I have my doubts that I have it in me to go through with it. As if reading my mind Henry tries to dispel my misgivings by smiling and reaching out for my hand. "Look at us drinking at lunch time! We will be alcoholics by the time we are let out! And then murderers a few months after that, fingers crossed."

Before all this, I used to sneak the occasional glass of wine with my lunch, but it is unlike Henry to be drinking.

He has always had a thing about people who drink too much, and used to make remarks about my drinking, although I do not like to go over twenty units a week ... Well, not often. I know the government says that fourteen units should be the limit, but that really isn't realistic, is it?

"You okay, Henry?" I ask.

Henry looks startled when I ask him this – you'd think I never ask him how he is. Perhaps I don't do it often enough.

"What do you mean? I have always hated Brian. I just think that as you're incapable of cutting him out of your life, the only option is to kill him. The bugger will live to at least a hundred otherwise. And after what he did to Daisy, death is too good for him ..."

"No, I am not talking about wanting to kill Dad. I am talking about you. You've changed. What's with all this shouting at the radio during the day, the sudden need for meditation and now a taste for wine during the day? This isn't the Henry I have been living with for over thirty years. I hope you're not having an affair ... It seems to be all the rage after all ..."

"Oh, Laura, chance would be a fine thing!" laughs Henry. "It is just that I am struggling with this whole lockdown, and my novel has hit a dead end."

Henry's novel is partly inspired by the two middle-aged friends of Henry's – friends who used to be part of both of our lives – who have recently walked out of their marriages, the two Pauls. The book is about a tragic affair, he tells me, that ends up destroying the lives of not just the protagonists, but many others around them.

"What's the problem?" I ask.

"I am sticking too closely to the truth – I'm describing what has actually happened. I know I should disguise it in some way, but I find that when I try and make things up, it

Chapter Eight

doesn't have the same authenticity. If this ever gets published, we are going to be dropped by all our friends."

"They aren't our friends, Henry. I have nothing to do with the Pauls anymore"

Henry has been friends with both Pauls since the kids were small. They are part of his quiz team that meets up every week, or did, before the COVID-19 thing happened. Now they have a regular online quiz every Thursday evening.

I used to be friends with both Pauls and their wives, too, but since the affairs, which came out in the open a couple of years ago, Henry has stuck by the husbands, whilst I have drifted apart from their exes. I kept having arguments with Henry about who was most in the wrong. It seems obvious to me it has to be the philanderers, but in Henry's view, the wives were just as much, if not more, to blame. I don't want other people's marriages falling apart to cause our own to disintegrate.

I try to console Henry: "You still have loads of other friends. There are Charlotte and Martin for starters."

"Yes, Charlotte is a true friend."

A wistful look appears on Henry's face, but maybe I am imagining it. I have never completely got rid of the feeling that I am a poor second to Charlotte, and if she hadn't dumped him all those years ago, he would still be with her. I wouldn't blame him – she is much more exciting than I have ever been. Where Charlotte is all bright colours and joyful laughter, I am more muted in every way. Henry has never made me feel second best; it is all my own paranoia ... I should really have let go of it by now.

I then do my best to reassure Henry further about the novel: "It is so hard to get published these days, and if some publisher does spot your brilliance, surely you can worry about how to tell your friends after? None of them are big readers – they will probably never find out!"

Henry laughs, but it is not a hearty laugh – more of a short bark, a laugh of despair. "Yes, here's hoping, Laura. I am never going to get it published so I need never worry about hurting anyone."

"That's not what I said at all! But why worry about something that may never happen?"

"Yes, Laura, I get your point. Look, I'd better get back to it. I may as well write whatever the hell I like, as no one is ever going to read it."

"I'll read it!" I say.

"You're always so supportive," says Henry, which I think is true, so I'm not sure why he is saying it in a slightly sarcastic tone. I decide that it is time for me to stop talking, as I don't seem to be helping.

It is time to get back to work, and work means being painstakingly accurate. That glass of wine was a bad idea.

Chapter Nine

Ninth sign of a psychopath: exploitative behaviour

Laura

Now over thirty-nine thousand deaths due to COVID in the UK.

As I work through the complex accounts of Dave Chapman, I see that things are not going well. I am not sure his business is going to survive all this. I worry about how he will be able to pay the redundancies that will be inevitable, and whether he will be eligible to apply to the government for more assistance. There is no point agonising over it now; I'll deal with that when it comes to it. Whenever lockdown eventually ends. Will it ever end? It is now flaming June, or rather showery June as it is turning out.

We are so lucky that we do not have money issues. I still need to work, well at least until I have sorted out Dad's estate, and then I can be a lady of leisure, a veritable Lady Macbeth of leisure. As long as I have the guts to carry out the plan.

I have shared it with Henry and he is behind me all the way. The only subject that Henry seems to get excited about these days is when I talk about killing Dad. I think he must be depressed – the lockdown is getting to him. I suppose he must be missing socialising; he is much more sociable than I am.

Saying that, over the last few weeks he has been managing to get out on his bike and go on long bike rides with his mates. There must be a group of about ten he regularly sees. Including the two philanderers, of course. They need to keep in shape now that they have younger partners to hold on to ...

I find it all so gross.

* * *

Dad's justification for his affairs was that one woman was never enough for him. He deserved some "fun" because he worked so hard. Dad has achieved a lot, there is no denying it. He loves to describe his rags-to-riches story. His father worked hard to make a living as a greengrocer working in the local market, but Dad went on to earn a fortune from working the stock market. Working in the greengrocer's trade from early on gave him some useful skills.

First, he learnt that if you can get away with a con, you must get away with a con. When he was young, until the age of ten or so, he used to walk out of Covent Garden where they got their trade fruit and veg with trays of produce that hadn't been paid for. His father reckoned he could get away with it because he was just a kid. And he did get away with it, until he grew too big to look innocent.

Dad also learnt to add up quickly in his head, so that he could tell customers how much their bags of shopping came

Chapter Nine

to and give them the right change. He would always charge a bit more than he should if he thought it was unlikely to be noticed.

I assume he must have used his skills at bamboozling people with figures in his work. And even after he had made lots of money, he still liked to pull a fast one if he could.

The first time I was aware of him trying to get away with something dodgy was when I was about six. We were visiting a National Trust property, and Dad wanted to pretend that he was a member but had forgotten his card. As we drove through the gates, Dad turned to me and said, "Don't say a word! When I say we have forgotten our cards, I don't want to hear a peep out of you."

This was a con that Dad failed to get away with, which meant he was cross for the whole day and kept going on about how much the visit was costing him and what a rip-off it was.

Dad also has a few objects in his house that he has somehow "acquired" from various posh places where he has either stayed or worked. There are some statuettes, a strange adding machine (that apparently is worth thousands), and even an oil painting. One of his favourite stories is how clever he was to he walk out with that under his arm, taking it from his office as though he had every right to, and not one person had dared to question him.

On the tours of his house, Dad liked to point out the items that he thought were worth the most. "Don't just let any house clearance people get their hands on any of this. You need to contact different auction houses and make sure you get the best price. Then of course there is my coin collection ..."

The coin collection! Naturally, if the thing you love most in the world (after yourself) is money, then it makes sense to collect it in every way you can. On his many tours of his treasures, Dad shows me his jars of old pennies, his trays of various coins, making me swear that I will go through it all when he dies and not just let some greedy coin expert give me a paltry lump sum for the whole lot. Which is exactly what will happen, I expect.

Chapter Ten

Tenth sign of a psychopath: lack of empathy

Laura

Hurrah! Now the travel restrictions are lifted, we can go back to our house on the Isle of Wight at last.

Henry's routine each morning is to have breakfast around seven-thirty and then bring me a coffee at eight, when I am usually still fast asleep. This morning, however, I find myself wide awake early and go downstairs to surprise Henry, thinking we can have breakfast together for a change.

"What are you doing up so early?" is his grumpy greeting.

"I am supposed to be the bad tempered one in the morning, not you!" I say, pulling a face. "I just woke up – maybe it's because it is already so hot in our bedroom. If you want to have your breakfast in peace, shall I take my breakfast outside?" I might be offering to eat separately for

Henry's sake, but actually I would rather be on my own if he is going to be off with me.

Henry sighs. "No of course not, sorry. I shouldn't listen to Radio 4 first thing. The constant news about the virus is getting me down. Will it never end?"

Desperate to keep things light and relieved it isn't my presence that is upsetting Henry, I babble on. "I haven't heard the news for days now, perhaps that is why I am in a strangely good mood. How about I make us both a cooked breakfast for a treat?"

Another sigh from Henry. "Thanks, but no thanks, Laura. I'll just stick to porridge. Want some?"

"Oh, as you're making it, yes please!"

There is a third sigh from Henry. But I try not to take it personally.

Once we are sitting down at the table, I rather regret letting Henry make porridge, as it is such a boring breakfast. Not worth the two hundred and seventy-five calories. I stop trying to make conversation, as it is going down as well with Henry as his porridge is going down with me. As soon as Henry has finished eating, he pushes his bowl away and – wait – Is that a small smile I see?

Then he starts an actual conversation, and a good one at that: "So shall I book the ferry tickets? When would you like to go? Do the kids want to come?"

"Amazingly, they do. They both say they want to have a few days on the beach. After all the hard work they claim to have been doing. I was thinking we could all go say Friday, and then us two could stay for ten days maybe, and Daisy and George could come back on the train after a long weekend."

"Ten days seems a long time."

"What? I thought you loved Bembridge?"

Chapter Ten

"Yes, but a week would be enough right now. It's hard to write there. And I want to finish the first draft whilst I am in the zone."

"Glad to hear you're in the zone. Is the novel going better now?"

Henry suddenly gets up and starts clearing the table. "Well, I am producing lots of words each day; whether they are any good is another matter. Anyway, I'll book the ferry whilst I'm at my desk, going out Friday and back the next Friday. The kids can sort out their own return journeys."

It will be so nice to see the sea. Surely Henry and I will be able to spend more time together when we are away? It is surprising how little time we actually spend together at the moment, as we work in separate rooms, exercise at different times ... I often only see him at dinnertime and after that he never wants to watch TV with me in the evening. He says I am a TV addict, but there isn't anything else to do. Well, nothing I fancy doing anyway ... Perhaps I should take up a hobby besides plotting Dad's death.

***

As a child I would have been a TV addict if that had been an option, but there wasn't enough TV to be addicted to during the day back in the 1960s and '70s. In the school holidays I had nothing to do – Dad would be at work and Mum would usually be lying down somewhere. She was always tired. Being awake during the day seemed to be a form of torture for her. Actually, just being alive seemed to be a torture for her, poor mum.

I would try and amuse myself, but not very hard, and would end up sitting in front of the TV. Watching the inanimate test card – my favourite was the one with a picture of a young girl in the middle playing noughts and crosses on a chalkboard with her weird-looking toy clown – until kids' programmes started up in the afternoon.

Occasionally, Mum would come and join me, with a drink in hand, and watch afternoon TV at the weekend if there was a film on. Those moments were special for me, as Mum wasn't there much in my childhood. Even when she was around, she was still absent. So watching a film with her was as good as it could get, in terms of engaging with her.

We watched Bette Davis films – her favourite. She also loved the film *Brief Encounter*, during which I even made her laugh, by imitating the posh accents of the children in the film as they spoke about their darling "Deady".

"Deady!" I'd say, copying the way they said "Daddy."

And then Mum would crack a joke: "I wish yours was Deady!" Though, thinking about it now, it probably wasn't a joke.

Whenever I think of Mum, I always think *poor Mum*. She wasn't a happy woman. When I'd ask Dad why Mum was so sad, Dad would say that she had never recovered from the trauma of my birth, so I thought it was my fault.

Now, with hindsight, I realise how wrong it was to blame myself for being the source of Mum's misery. Especially after what she said to me at the end.

The end. It wasn't a happy ending. Mum had always self-medicated with alcohol and Valium, and eventually it caught up with her. Considering how much she drank, it's amazing she lasted as long as she did. She was seventy-five when she died – five years ago now.

Her death wasn't an easy one. She was in a lot of pain, despite the amount of morphine being pumped into her, as her organs gave up one by one. Those afternoons sitting with her in the hospitals were grim. I suggested to Dad that he at least pay for a nicer room, somewhere with a window view, maybe, but he wasn't willing to shell out for private healthcare.

A few days before she died, Mum gripped my hand hard. So hard I had to gently loosen her fingers a little. It was her last show of strength.

"Laura!" Her voice sounded urgent. Perhaps these were going to be her last words?

"What is it, Mum?" I leant towards her. What she said next surprised me. You know how you hope that your mum or dad will finally say the words you have always longed to hear? Well, she said them.

"I love you, Laura."

Stunned, I squeezed her hand.

"I love you, too, Mum."

"I'm sorry, Laura."

"I'm sorry, too, Mum."

When Mum gripped my hand hard again, I did not adjust her grip, worried I would interrupt her flow. She spoke slowly and deliberately, putting all her effort into every syllable.

"No, Laura. What I did was wrong.

Very wrong.

I should have left him.

I should have protected you from him.

Don't let him ruin the rest of your life."

I didn't reply, just kept holding onto Mum's hand.

Mum kept staring at me, not dropping her gaze.

"Promise me, Laura. Promise me, Laura."

I looked straight back. "I promise, Mum."

And now, at last, I am going to keep that promise. Soon, I hope, he will be Deady.

Chapter Eleven

Eleventh sign of a psychopath: excessive self-absorption

Henry

The first draft of the book is finished, but I don't feel like celebrating. As I have been writing about the deaths of the fictional marriages in my novel, I feel like I have also been describing the death of my own marriage.

I had hoped that this trip to our house by the sea would be good for us all. Everyone else is having a great time, especially Jeff. Part of my malaise is down to yet another mouth ulcer and now I have an awful earache. I am having to take even stronger painkillers than usual.

This morning, Daisy and George are in their rooms, and I don't expect to see them until midday at the earliest. I was planning to take Jeff for a walk on the beach on my own, but when Laura realises where I am going, she says, "Wait! I'll come with you". The last time we walked the dog together, I

Chapter Eleven

realise, is the last time we were here, way back in February. Before the world went mad. Before we went crazy and decided to put an end to Brian.

As we head down to the beach, Jeff becomes drunk on the joy of being by the sea. The minute we arrive at the shingle he almost strangles himself trying to escape from his lead and get into the water. I have to let him have freedom, and as soon as I unclip him, he is off, running straight into the sea, playing with the waves, yapping with joy.

I wish I could be that happy. And then I am surprised to hear Laura echo my thoughts and say: "I wish I could be that happy."

"Aren't you happy, Laura?"

Laura laughs and shakes her head. "No one can be as happy as a dog on a beach. I'm fine. I'm lucky. As long as we are all healthy, I have nothing to complain about. Apart from you know who. But we should be sorting that problem out soon."

I wait for Laura to ask me if I'm happy. But she falls silent.

It is not surprising that Laura doesn't ask me that often about how I am feeling. I am always taken aback when she does. She hasn't been trained to be interested in the minutiae of other people's inner lives. Her parents never showed much interest in hers. She told me that when she rang her mum up to tell her she had succeeded in getting a 2:1 in her maths degree, her mum said: "Oh! We didn't know you were doing a degree!" Even though Laura had been away for three years at Bristol, her parents had never given a thought as to what she might be doing there.

I, on the other hand, was at home when I got my results. I had been picked up by my dad from my disgusting student house in Coventry as soon as I had finished my course. It had taken him three hours to drive up from Southampton. He then helped me stuff all my bin bags full of records, clothes, and mugs into his trusty old Ford Cortina and drive the three hours back home. I took it for granted that my parents would look after me. I didn't realise how lucky I was until I met Laura's parents.

When I got my results – a 2:2 – Mum and Dad both cried. I was the first person in the family to go to uni, though I am probably the most stupid one out of the lot of us. A few years later, my sister, Polly, completely eclipsed me by going to Oxford to study psychology. She is still eclipsing me – you have probably heard her expounding on about her book *Our Secret Lives* on Radio 4.

Polly and I always got on okay when we were young, but we have drifted apart. I don't think it is just because she blames me for the death of our parents.

We'd already had an emotional distance between us before the nightmare accident. Polly appeared horrified by our children when they came along, as she seems to be by all kids. She likes to lead an orderly life in Oxford as an academic, where she has always lived since she was a student. Her book is aptly named, as I think she manages to keep her life private and shows zero interest in ours now.

Then there is the issue of the cottage in Bembridge, which has also caused a few – well, I wouldn't call them fights, but awkward exchanges of emails. We divide our time equally there, but sometimes we both want to go at the same time. Now I just let her have first dibs; it just isn't worth the aggro. A few years ago, her emails almost became vitriolic when I asked if we could spend New Year's there, though it wasn't our turn. I then suggested that maybe we could all go down together. She wrote something along the

Chapter Eleven

lines that if she wanted to have an awful time with some smug family, our family was certainly not one that would be top of her list.

Even before all the awfulness of losing Mum and Dad, even before the kids came along, Polly lost interest in me once I started going out with Laura. I asked her at the time if she didn't like Laura. "Of course not," she replied. "What is there not to like?" – giving the impression that there was nothing much to like either.

The shock of the car crash that killed Mum and Dad hit me just as hard as it hit Polly. They were driving to ours for Christmas when the kids still believed in Father Christmas. When Christmases at our house were full of fun ... When they were worth making a trip for.

"You shouldn't haves asked them!" Polly shouted at me in the hospital. "You know what Dad's driving is like. And in this weather, the motorway is like an ice rink. I nearly had an accident getting here myself!" Although we had both raced to the hospital on admittedly treacherous roads, Polly did not make it in time to say goodbye to Mum or Dad. Mum had died in the ambulance before she got to the hospital, but I just made it in time to hold Dad's hand before he lost consciousness. Polly held that against me too.

I do not accept any blame for the death of our parents. When Brian dies, then, yes, plenty of blame can be placed on me, although the true blame lies with him. There are many reasons why the world would be a better place without Brian; there are many reasons why we will be better off, financially and mentally, without that monster in our lives.

I don't want Brian dead because of the inheritance, though I admit it is the money that will allow me to leave without disrupting the lives of Laura, Daisy, and George too much. The reason I want him dead is because he put his nasty hands on Daisy. In my head, there is no other recourse but to finish him off. If I could do it slowly and painfully, I would. Laura's plan means he should go more quickly than he deserves, though not completely without pain.

Chapter Twelve

Twelfth sign of a psychopath: expecting and
wanting everyone to be envious of them

Laura

The COVID fatality rate seems to be plateauing, but with over forty thousand deaths in the UK, this is little comfort. I cannot think about each individual loss; there are too many people affected for my mind to cope with. I have to switch off.

It helped to get away, and not think about the news for a week. Even though the four of us have been stuck together since the start of lockdown, somehow it felt we were properly together when we were in our seaside cottage.

The long walks, the meals out (meals out – such a treat after so many months without them!) meant we talked much more than usual. I feel so blessed with my family – they are all so nice. "Nice" is a damning word, I know, but nice is what they are. And it is so "nice" to be with them all.

I was feeling that Henry was drifting away from us all

for a while, but I realise now it was just because he was so immersed in his novel. He still seems a million miles away sometimes, but then, he often has. Always so cerebral, I suppose that is what happens if you have a good imagination. For me it has been a real strain imagining the future and visualising a properly viable plan for killing Dad, even though I have been obsessed with getting rid of him for years. The plan seems solid, but I still can't believe we have the mental strength to go through with it.

All through lockdown I have hoped Dad would just drop down dead suddenly, so we wouldn't have to do the deed ourselves. Meanwhile, many people we know are mourning the loss of parents who have died over this period.

Here are the ways they have died:

Coronavirus – a mother of one of my bridge partners died at the end of March and a friend of Henry's dad died last week.

A fatal accident – a neighbour's dad was hit by a car on the main road outside Boots in Twickenham.

Old age – one of Henry's cycling mates recently lost his ninety-nine-year-old dad. He just didn't wake up one morning. The way we would all like to go.

I have tried method one already to turn Daddy to Deady. Method three is never going to happen, but I am thinking about ways I could booby trap Dad's house when I next go there – worth a try before we attempt our current murder plan as that can't happen before October and it would be good to get this sorted before then.

I am due to do the weekly shop for Dad this afternoon, so today could be the day.

Before I go, I heat up some soup. I call out from the kitchen that lunch is ready, but no reply. I call again, and get a shout from George's room: "I told you I want to make my own lunch!"

"Where's Dad?" I shout back.

"How the hell should I know?"

Daisy isn't in; she's staying with her boyfriend, Ben, which isn't strictly allowed, but when I voiced my concerns I got shouted down, so I gave up. To be honest, it is nice to have her out the house – she's in a permanent bad mood these days. She is lovely though, really. This whole lockdown with the family must have been very stressful for her. Not how a twenty-year-old wants to live.

I go on the hunt for Henry. First, I look in the garden, which is tiny, so it is easy to see there is no one there. Then I climb up the stairs to our bedroom to find Henry sitting on the yoga mat with headphones on.

"Lunch!" I say.

Henry takes off the headphones. "Sorry, was listening to a meditation podcast."

"How very Zen of you."

Henry smiles, appropriately with a kind of Buddha-like serene smile, but says nothing.

At the table, I outline my kill-Dad-right-now plan.

"So I was thinking that if I pour some oil on the bathroom floor that could work ..."

Henry nods. "Worth a try, but what sort of oil? Why would there be oil on a bathroom floor?"

"It could be some sort of scented oil, I suppose, or essential oil ..."

Henry frowns. "I'm not sure. Brian is sure to notice a big pool of scented oil on the floor, and he would know it would have had to be you that put it there ... Surely it would make more sense to pour olive oil on his kitchen floor, paved as it is with those expensive stone tiles?"

"He has also got that massive Aga. It would be really nasty if he hit his head on that ..."

"You want to make sure that no one else could slip on it instead of him. You don't want to kill someone else by mistake. You know how he likes to get people to come round and do stuff for him."

This is a good point. It would be awful if his cleaner Teresa had an accident. I know she comes on Mondays, and today is Wednesday, so she should be safe. But I must make sure that Dad is the first person to go in the kitchen after I have laid my deadly trap.

The dropping off of Dad's shopping follows its usual pattern. I carry all the stuffed carrier bags into the kitchen and then Dad unpacks them with his usual *harrumph*s and grunts.

"I'll just knock £10 off this week, Laura, as you have gone to Waitrose again, but would it really be so difficult to make an effort to save some of your money by going to Lidl? And I don't know why you insist on using these nasty cotton bags. Plastic seems much more hygienic,"

"I'm trying to save the planet, Dad."

"I think it is too late for that," Dad says.

"Yes, sadly I think you're right."

Then comes the usual: "Before you go, Laura ...."

Which means it must be time to head upstairs to be stared at by his portraits whilst we go through the will again.

Dad walks out the kitchen, expecting me to follow, but I linger.

Dad calls out: "What are you doing still in the kitchen?"

"Just washing my hands, Dad!"

I am not washing my hands, but pouring a glug of cooking oil in a strategic spot between the sink and the Aga.

Chapter Twelve

Surely he can't miss this? And then I use a cloth to spread it around so it isn't too obvious.

Dad calls out again: "Hurry up, Laura! What's taking you so long?"

"Sorry Dad, coming!"

And then I do something incredibly stupid. I slip.

I scream as I fall and thud down.

I have slipped so that I fall backwards, and I put my arms out behind me so that I land quite safely, though heavily, on my hands and then my bottom.

Dad calls out again, "What's going on, Laura?"

"I fell over!"

"Stupid woman! Stop making a fuss and come up here!"

I gingerly get up and make my way out of the kitchen, being much more careful where I step this time.

When I get up to the study, Dad says, "How come you fell over? You getting old before your time, Laura?"

"These socks I'm wearing are a bit slippy," I reply.

"Maybe the floor is too polished; Terry does too thorough a job sometimes. I occasionally wonder if she makes the floor slippy on purpose, hoping to trip me up."

Dad bellows with laughter, but I wonder if he is right – maybe Teresa wants to get rid of him too.

"Do me a favour and make sure the kitchen is safe before you leave. I can't risk falling over myself. If you give it a quick wipe over with a mop and some detergent, that should do the trick."

Before we go through the usual will rigmarole, Dad's phone rings. He picks up the handset, looks at the screen, and a sneer crosses his face before he places the phone back down without answering it.

"Who is that you don't want to talk to?"

"Geoffrey again. He's beginning to get on my nerves," says Dad.

"Be a shame to fall out with Geoffrey," I say. "He's your oldest friend."

"Yes, he is getting old, though I know that is not what you meant exactly. Old people are a bloody nuisance in my opinion."

And in my opinion too as it happens, when it comes to Dad anyway.

After going through the usual discussion about his will, Dad leans back in his chair, the expression on his face one I recognise all too well. He is about to start a marathon of boasting about all his financial brilliant coups of the past. I plant the usual fake-interested expression on my face and prepare to drift off into my own world, imagining how bad an accident Dad could have in the kitchen. What would happen if he only got injured, broke a leg or something? Would that mean he would become more demanding than ever? Should I abandon my plan?

My reverie is broken by a bark from Dad: "Am I boring you again, Laura. Am I a terrible bore?"

"No, of course not, Dad, you just make me feel like such a failure in comparison ..."

I have learnt over the years this is the only correct response to Dad's boasting.

"Yes, it is a shame, Laura, but the genes don't always get passed down. At least you will benefit from my wheeler-dealing eventually, when I am gone ..."

Again, I give a response that I have been trained to give: "Oh, I don't know, Dad. You're so fit that you will probably outlive me."

Having done my daughterly duty in the study, I let Dad

Chapter Twelve

lead me to the cupboard downstairs, so that I can fulfil my cleaning duty in the kitchen.

"Here you go, the mop and bucket are in here."

I decide not to do any mopping but spend time in the kitchen making sure there is still enough grease on the floor to be dangerous.

Soon after I get home, Dad calls.

"You idiot, Laura! You must be the worst cleaner in the world!"

Then I hear my Dad's loud laughter – he can't believe how stupid his daughter is. Eventually, he stops laughing enough to bark out: "You missed a huge patch of oil on the kitchen floor. So much for your mopping. Maybe your eyesight is failing! Lucky I have got such great eyesight or I could have had a nasty accident. I had to ask Jim next door to come over and sort it out." More laughter. "You must be one of the most useless women in the world. I dread to think of the state your house must be in."

I am certainly useless when it comes to finishing off Dad. I will damn well make sure the next attempt is the final one.

I am speaking to Dad on my mobile in the front living room, much to the annoyance of Henry, who has been trying to watch some old tennis match on the TV, which he pointedly mutes whilst I am on the phone. As soon as I end the call, instead of switching the sound back on, Henry turns off the TV altogether. Oh no, I am going to get it in the neck from him, too. Why is he so cross?

I soon find out.

"So I gather that your plan went wrong today?" Henry asks.

"Actually, Henry," I say, trying to defuse his bad mood by sharing the comedy of what happened earlier, "it went spectacularly wrong! Not only did I not kill Dad, I nearly killed myself! I fell over on the oily trap I set and landed flat on my behind."

Henry does not laugh.

"This is not some comedy farce, Laura. We are not playing games here. Do you really want to kill Brian, or are you just going to make half-hearted attempts? Have you got it in you to take it to the next level? If you're not taking this seriously, then let me know. That man has to be punished. If you aren't serious about ending his life, tell me and I'll take care of it myself."

Henry has a point. So much of my mental energy has been spent hating Dad and imagining life without him and ways of getting rid of him that I'm used to having these thoughts and living with them. If I really wanted to kill him, then surely I would have found a way, or at least found a way of living without Dad by cutting him out of my life. What am I playing at?

"I'm sorry, Henry. I need to think. You're right – it is no good having a perfect plan for murdering Dad if I haven't got the guts to carry it out."

Henry's expression softens and he takes my hand: "I'm here, you're not doing this on your own. I will be with you every step of the way. Remember what this man has done to you, how he treated your mum and the unforgivable things he has done to girls, including our own Daisy. If, after you have thought about this – properly thought about this – then let me know. Because I mean it, Laura, if you can't face doing this on your own, then I will take care of it."

Chapter Thirteen

Thirteenth sign of a psychopath: arrogant behaviour

Laura

When I read on the BBC news site that the way deaths from coronavirus are counted in England has reduced the UK death toll by more than five thousand, to forty-one thousand, three hundred and twenty-nine, I wasn't sure what to believe. Massaging figures has never been my strength, which is probably not what you want from an accountant.

To get away from dwelling on depressing statistics, it is a real treat after all those months in lockdown to go out for dinner with other people instead of just the family. Tonight I have booked a table at our favourite local French restaurant with Charlotte and Martin.

Just as I'm running a bath, Daisy comes into the bathroom.

"No, Mum, you can't have a bath now; I said I was going to have one."

"But I have to get ready, we are leaving in half an hour."

"That's not my problem," says Daisy. "I told you this morning I needed the bathroom at six. I've got to dye my hair."

"Okay, fine," I say and turn around to leave.

"There is no need to be so passive aggressive!" says Daisy. "This is not a big deal. You don't need to bath all the time ..."

"I said fine, and I'm not being passive aggressive. Look at me! This is just my normal facial expression, one of calm acceptance ..."

"Not calm acceptance at all. It is your normal make-my-family-feel-guilty expression," finishes Daisy.

My kids are always saying I try to make them feel guilty, but if that was so, how come they never do? That is unfair – they have nothing to feel guilty about. They are great kids. I'm the one with issues, I remind myself.

In the bedroom Henry is getting ready and I complain to him that either the kids need to move out, or we need to get another bathroom.

"We can't afford another bathroom. We generally manage fine," says Henry.

"Well, when this is all over, when we do come into some money," I say, "we should get some work done on the house."

"That's a long time away, so let's not discuss it now."

Henry is buttoning up a rather nice shirt I haven't seen him wear before, bright blue crisp cotton. He looks kind of depressed, I think, but maybe that is just how his face looks now that he is in his late fifties. People are always asking me why I'm looking so sad these days, and I'm sure it is just because my face is beginning to sag.

Chapter Thirteen   85

In the restaurant, I start to change my mind about Henry. It is not just old age that is making him look miserable; he really is miserable.

Charlotte is full of chat as usual, dominating the conversation with her tales of lockdown domestic life. Sounds like everyone has gone stir crazy in her house over the last three months, apart from Scratchy, who has been having a ball.

"Jeff the Dog has been having the best time too," I say.

When we have all finished eating, Charlotte turns her attention to Henry, as he has hardly said a word. "How has it been for you, Henry? I hear you are writing a novel?"

"It has been strange for me as for everyone else," says Henry. "And the novel is finished."

"Want to tell us about it?" asks Charlotte.

"Not really, no," says Henry, which I think is a bit rude, so I try to add some explanation as to why Henry is being so uncommunicative. Usually he lights up when Charlotte speaks, as do most people.

"Things have been difficult in our house, what with the kids being so loud and getting in our way when Henry and I are trying to work. And I feel a bit sick all the time. I think it must be underlying anxiety."

Charlotte nods. "It might be your dad upsetting you again. He has been extra demanding lately."

"Yes," I reply, "but I find I'm obsessing about him too much. I was thinking I should speak to someone about it, maybe find a therapist ..."

At this point Henry throws down his napkin, stands up and says, "Sorry everyone, I'm feeling weird, I have to go." He leaves so quickly he doesn't stop to grab his jacket.

Embarrassing.

Martin tries to come to the rescue. He picks up Henry's

jacket lying next to him and gets up himself. "I'll just go and see if I can catch up with him and find out if he wants to go for a drink ... I'll leave you two to it ..."

Once he has gone, Charlotte and I quickly settle the bill. Before we leave, she calls Martin to find out he has ended up going to a bar with Henry.

"Shall we join them?" she asks.

The last thing I want to do is join them. Charlotte might be acting like everything is normal, but I feel completely humiliated. Martin would never abandon her in a restaurant. He would never create a scene. What has got into Henry? I am too furious with him to go and act like nothing out of the ordinary has happened. I try to keep my voice light, I don't want Charlotte to see how shaken I am.

"I think it will be good for Henry to talk to someone else, without me there. Maybe Martin will get to the bottom of what's wrong ..."

"Don't be ridiculous," says Charlotte. "Martin never likes to talk about anything more than sport and music; he only talks about such subjects as complicated as feelings with me, and that is only if I force him too. You're lucky that Henry is so open about everything. You want to go for a drink, just the two of us?"

"Actually, I'd like to get home ..."

"Great, that's what I'd like too. I should get it to myself for an hour or so as the boys are out. I can catch up on some crap TV."

Henry gets home about two hours after I do. He smells of beer but seems in a much better mood. I don't want a fight, so I don't say anything immediately, just switch off the TV. I had been trying to distract myself with something light – *First Dates* is one of my guilty pleasures.

Chapter Thirteen

"Sorry about walking out," Henry says as he shuts the lounge door. "And it was nice being with Martin. I don't often get to see him on his own."

"Yes, he and Charlotte make a great couple." I am talking for the sake of it, trying to keep things light.

However, I seem to have hit a nerve as Henry frowns when I say this. I don't want to find out why he is frowning; I couldn't bear to have my suspicions confirmed that Henry doesn't think anyone is good enough for Charlotte. That Henry still has feelings for Charlotte after all these years. I decide to change the subject and tackle the more immediate problem, which is what made Henry act so badly this evening.

"Why did you storm out?"

"I didn't exactly storm out. I couldn't stand the idea of you getting a therapist. I think we have discussed your dad enough. I think you're just looking to talk to someone else as a way of getting out of the situation. What are you going to tell them? That you want to kill your dad? Hope they will offer another solution?"

"Yes, of course I want another solution, Henry! Do we really want to become murderers?"

Henry raises his arm. Is he going to hit me? No, of course not; he would never do that. I realise he is only raising it to rest it against the wall. I think he is finding it hard to stand up ... He must be more drunk than he appears.

"Let me remind you, Laura – though I shouldn't need to – why we are doing this."

* * *

Dad had told us last July that Christmas was to be at his house. He wanted us and the kids to come over so he would not have to drive and therefore could drink as much as he liked. It was a recent decision of his to give up driving whilst under the influence. We were to bring over the food, as it would be too much for him to cook the dinner as well as host us.

Henry said that we should refuse to see him, but I said that as unpleasant as it was to spend time with Dad, it was only one day, and we hadn't spent Christmas with him for years.

Before they died, we had always invited Henry's parents over. Every other year, I would invite my parents over too. I used to invite Polly too, but she would only come if my parents were not going to be joining us. I didn't blame her. Henry's parents were obviously not keen on my parents either, judging from the looks of horror I saw fleeting across their faces whenever Dad told one of his boastful stories. I would also note Henry's mum's lips pursing a little as Mum poured herself yet another drink.

The day started off badly at Dad's and got worse. When we arrived at lunchtime, it was clear Dad had been drinking for a while. He opened the door when we arrived without saying a word, which was very unusual for him, and then wove his way back into his sitting room. He tried to sit down on an armchair, but missed it, landing on the floor.

"Bloody Teresa moving all the furniture around!" he said as he pulled himself up.

When I went into the dining room, I was surprised to see the table had been laid with a fantastic central arrangement of dried holly, ivy, and poinsettias sprayed gold and lavishly placed in a bronze vase.

"Wow!" I called out. "The table looks amazing!"

"Only because I told Terry what to do," Dad shouted back.

Chapter Thirteen

This was more like the Christmases I remembered – Dad had obviously got his voice back.

"When was Teresa over?"

"Yesterday," yelled Dad.

"Good of her to work Christmas Eve."

"Well, she enjoys it. She likes being servile," Dad screamed back. "Anyway, what you doing in there? You should be in the kitchen shouldn't you? The food isn't going to cook itself I assume?"

I went into the kitchen to heat up everything we had brought. I had precooked it all – even the Brussel sprouts, which I had roasted with garlic and rosemary. Exactly seven sprouts each, which I take as a good sign as I hadn't counted them before I cooked them. George and Daisy had made themselves a nut roast and I had prepared a large chicken, as Dad says turkey is for "losers".

Henry came into the kitchen after about five minutes. "Give me strength, I can't take him even when he's pissed."

He was soon followed by George. "I'll make the gravy, Mum. You always mess it up."

During the meal, Dad seemed to sober up somewhat, huffing and puffing over how badly I had cooked the meal. "What have you done to the sprouts?" ... "This gravy tastes odd, is it vegetarian? That must be why it's so tasteless" ... "Just as well your mum isn't still alive, she'd be horrified at how you have massacred this chicken."

I wanted to reply that Mum never cared about anything she ate, because she always picked at her food, getting most of her calories from wine and vodka. But I didn't want to start an argument. Dad was itching for a fight, though, as he kept saying things he thought would get me going, but I just smiled and said nothing. Eventually he exploded, slammed his hand down on the table and demanded: "What's wrong with you all? So bloody quiet! this is supposed to be Christmas – don't any of you have anything interesting to say? What a useless lot you all are, I hope at least one of you two kids amounts to something one day, unlike your parents!"

"I think it's time for the crackers, Dad," I said in a vain hope to move things in a more pleasant direction.

I failed.

In the car going home, at first we were all silent and then George started laughing, saying, "I think that has to win the prize as our worst Christmas family gathering ever!" His laughter started me off and soon I had tears rolling down my face and so did Henry. Daisy, however, kept silent. I looked back at her to see her staring fixedly out of the window.

"You okay, Daisy?"

"Fine," she replied, evidently not wanting to be drawn, so I left it.

When we got home, Daisy went straight up to her bedroom. When I made coffee for us all to have with mince pies, I called up to her, but no reply. I went upstairs and knocked on her door. Silence. I pushed the door open to find her lying face down on her bed, weeping silently.

That is when I found out what Dad did. The information that pushed our dreams of killing Dad into concrete plans.

Daisy told me that when we were all in the kitchen, Dad asked her to give her grandad a cuddle. So she went over to him to give him a hug around his shoulders but he grabbed her and pulled her into his lap. Before she could fight her way out of his grip, he managed to force his hand up her skirt. She managed to kick herself free, but was too

Chapter Thirteen

shocked and scared to scream or swear at him. She said she was paralysed, mentally and physically.

Dad had then said, "That's what happens to girls who wear short skirts, so be warned!" He started laughing at her. "You should see your shocked face, Daisy! And always pretending to be so cool. Well, you are cool – so cold that you are frigid I would say." More laughter.

Daisy said that at first she thought it was just some terrible Grandad joke, and felt maybe she was silly to be upset, but when she was in the car, some other memories came back to her. Glimpses of similar things happening in the past.

"He never made me touch him or anything, I don't think he ever really molested me; I just remember cuddles that were a bit uncomfortable."

"That *is* molesting you! He abused you!"

"I don't know, Mum, I don't feel molested; I just feel weird. Don't tell Dad."

"I have to tell Dad, Daisy. This can't be ignored. You will have been affected by this. You *are* affected by this. You should talk to a professional. We need to decide what to do."

Daisy then sat up and screamed at me, "Drop it, Mum! I want to forget about it!"

"Well, that's the last time you've seen your Grandfather, that is for certain. You will never have to put up with anything so traumatic again. I am so sorry, it's all my fault."

"Oh, stop being such a victim, Mum, it is not always about you. I wish I had never told you."

It was my fault, though. It is up to a mother to protect her kids and I failed. I didn't tell Henry that night. I didn't know what to do ... I couldn't sleep because the awful image of Dad hurting Daisy kept surfacing. I eventually dropped off around dawn, and was woken by Henry bringing me my coffee.

"Stay, Henry," I said. "I have something terrible to tell you."

Chapter Fourteen

Fourteenth sign of a psychopath: abnormal ways of thinking

Laura

I decide to ignore Henry's reaction to my idea of having some form of counselling. I find that I'm counting everything I do to such a compulsive level that I can't even get my head straight to do my work. And we can't afford for me to stop working. Not yet.

Apparently the UK is about to see a second wave of COVID infections. Will this ever end? As if I have some control, I stir my coffee exactly twenty times before drinking it. When I go down for breakfast, I count every stair and every step, because the total must come to fifty before I let myself sit down. I then place exactly five tablespoons of cereal into my bowl. And rather than pour the milk over it, I pour it carefully into a small measuring cup, so that I get exactly a third of a cup.

Counting everything is exhausting. Although I have always had a tendency to do it in the past, it has never been as bad as this. When I am on my walk in the park with Jeff the Dog, I call up Charlotte as soon as I get to exactly five thousand steps.

"It's started up again, the obsessive counting. You know you helped me stop doing it when were at school."

Charlotte laughs. "I didn't really do anything, apart from kick you when I knew you were doing it. A mad look used to come into your eye. You want me to come and meet you and give you a good kicking now?"

"No, that's okay, I think it is beyond that. I wonder if you could suggest a therapist who could help. Maybe that woman you went to when the kids were small and you were having panic attacks."

"I needed someone to sort out the kids really, but she was a help – just getting away from them sometimes did me the world of good. I'm not sure she would still be working; she was about seventy when I saw her. And anyway, you aren't supposed to go to the same therapists as your friends. But I have got a suggestion for you. Because it is still hard to see counsellors face to face, if you don't fancy seeing someone over a computer screen, why not try to find one of these walking therapists? They counsel you as you go on walks. You might even be able to take Jeff the Dog with you."

I glance at Jeff, who is straining on the lead which I always keep him on in Richmond Park after the deer incident. "I definitely will not be bringing Jeff, even though he is probably in more need of help than I am."

As I draw near the house I check my steps. Nine thousand and seventy. So I walk past the house until it reaches nine thousand, four hundred and thirty, then turn back. As I reach my front door it hits exactly ten thousand.

Finding a "walking" counsellor is straightforward. I

google walking therapy in Richmond and a name pops straight up, with a reassuring picture of Richmond Park. Jo Wong. I message her immediately before I can change my mind, and get an email back the same evening. After a quick video call where Jo finds out a bit about me and explains how the sessions work, our first appointment is booked for just two days' time at four pm. Which is forty-six hours and seventeen minutes away. Jo sends me some forms to fill in after our video call, which confirm the price (£55 an hour) and set out how the walks will take place. Looks like bringing Jeff the Dog is not an option, as I'm supposed to not even bring a bag or coffee cup.

Forty-six hours, twelve minutes later, I'm sitting on the agreed bench looking at the view of the river from the top of Richmond Hill. Five minutes later, Jo sits down at the other end of the bench. "Still not right to shake hands, so are you happy just to start walking?"

Jo is a bit younger than I would have chosen – I was hoping that maybe she looked younger on screen that she would in real life, but if anything she looks even younger, no more than forty at the most. I suppose at my age, most counsellors are likely to be younger than me.

We walk into Richmond Park, Jo making it clear that she will never invade my space by getting nearer than a metre to me. She also explains that I might well feel like crying as we talk, and that is perfectly natural. She can't reassure me physically, but she says she is always going to be right next to me supporting me and making sure that I'm being looked after.

Almost as soon as we have passed through the park gates, and veered onto the footpath towards the right, I start crying. Jo says nothing whilst tears pour out of me and I quickly get through three of the tissues I have brought (Jo had told me I needed to bring my own tissues).

After about ten minutes of this, Jo stops and says, "Just pause here for a minute. Look at the view …"

Although I have passed this viewpoint at least five hundred times (assuming I have come to this park once or twice a month since I moved to Richmond), and around fifty times since lockdown, I find that I haven't really taken in this view at all. You can see all the way to the spire of St Paul's Cathedral. It is a sunny day, so the roof of the cathedral shines white in the light.

I stop crying, and stare at the view. I say nothing for a while. And then: "Wow. London seems like another world away, and yet here you feel you could almost reach out your hand and touch it."

"Whatever you have going through your mind," Jo says, "no matter how bad you feel, it is important to stop sometimes and look. Really look. Examine everything you see, look at it through fresh eyes, as though you're an alien who has just landed on this planet. Too often we look inwards, and forget to look around us."

When we start walking again, and my crying has calmed down, Jo asks me what I have been crying about. "I don't know where to start."

"Pinpoint one person, or event, that comes to the front of your mind."

"My father," I say. Poor Jo, she is going to hear a lot about my dad. But I can't tell her I'm planning to kill him. If I tell her that, she would have to report me. This was very clear on the forms I filled in. They didn't specify murder of course, but any criminal activity that I'm planning would have to be reported, apparently.

This is not something to worry about now, however, as I

Chapter Fourteen

have so much to say about Dad and my childhood, that getting to the present and my feelings now is a long way off.

After a brief summary of the early years with my dad, and how I never liked being with him, Jo asks if I have any memory, even the smallest one, of anything positive about growing up.

So I tell her about my dog, Tootsie, who briefly made me very happy.

I had begged my parents for a dog, because my pretty friend Lucy had a border collie called Shep (named after the *Blue Peter* dog) that was the most brilliant animal I had ever met. Whenever I went to Lucy's house her dog was absolutely the highlight of the visit. He used to play fetch with us endlessly in her large garden, and was always wagging his tail and generally appearing thoroughly delighted to have us around.

On my eleventh birthday I was given my dream present. Mum took me to Battersea Dogs' Home and we met Tootsie, a mongrel who was as close to a border collie as we could find in there. Tootsie was only a few years old, a white dog with brown ears and a brown tail.

Tootsie didn't seem as happy a dog as Lucy's lovely Shep, but then she must have had a hard life, Mum explained, before she went into the home.

She might have been a morose dog, but I still adored Tootsie. I had promised faithfully before I got her that I would walk the dog every day. Not surprising, as Dad had said: "The first day you don't bother to walk your stupid dog is the last day of that dog's life, so be warned!"

I took his warnings seriously, and the only times that Tootsie would look excited was when I showed her her lead. Then she would jump up at me wagging her tail so hard I was worried it would fall off.

I produced Tootsie's lead in the morning before I went to school, and again as soon as I got home. I was also the person who fed her in the mornings. I reckon she hadn't been fed properly before because she would gobble up her food so quickly each morning, she would always start choking. It took about five seconds for her to get a whole tin of Pedigree Chum down her. It was a bit disgusting, really. Apart from her horrible eating, and her miserable persona when she wasn't on a walk, Tootsie was a lovely dog. Maybe not as fun as Shep or as lively, and she never took to playing fetch, but I adored her anyway.

I didn't adore her for long.

I got up early as usual one morning to take Tootsie for her walk in the park, but when I produced the lead, Tootsie didn't jump up as usual from her basket. She just lifted her head, looked at me as if to say, *I fancy a lie in this morning,* and then put it back down and shut her eyes.

"Walkies!" I said to try and encourage her. Tootsie briefly raised her head again and then put it back down.

I put the lead away. Dad was already at work and Mum was still in bed, so I left a note out on the kitchen table: *"Tootsie may not be well? Needs to go to the vet?"*

I was worried all day at school about Tootsie.

I was right to be worried. When I came home, the house was horribly quiet. No dog to greet me at the front door after I let myself in. No dog in the dog basket. No dog anywhere.

I found Mum lying on the settee in the lounge. "Where is Tootsie?"

Mum sat up straight away. "So sorry, Lucy ..."

Before she could tell me the whole story, I threw myself down on our expensive Turkish silk rug and started wailing.

When I had calmed down enough to listen, Mum

Chapter Fourteen

explained that Tootsie had left a poo right in the middle of the kitchen floor. When Mum had called Dad to ask him what to do, he had been very clear about what had to be done. And Mum had followed his instructions to the letter.

"She didn't suffer, Laura."

I screamed back, "Well I hope someone puts you down if you get a bad tummy!" And ran up the stairs to weep on my bed.

Mum eventually followed me up and stood in my bedroom doorway. "You said a very wicked thing, Laura, and I can't forgive you. These are the last words I am ever saying to you, Laura. You are no longer my daughter."

They weren't the very last words Mum spoke to me, obviously. But she didn't speak to me for at least a week.

After I have finished telling Jo about Tootsie, Jo says, "It is natural for a daughter to tell her mum she wants her dead sometimes. Your mum was wrong to make you feel it was unforgivable."

I feel a huge wave of relief go through me, just from hearing this simple sentence. A "professional" has at last recognised how rubbish my parents sometimes were.

I want to say: *So you can see why I have decided to kill my dad then*. But I stay silent.

Chapter Fifteen

Fifteenth sign of a psychopath: need for excessive respect

Henry

I have one extremely painful ulcer on my tongue. I've googled "recurrent mouth ulcers" but can't find an obvious reason. It might seem minor, but these ulcers are getting me down. Ageing also means I always have an ache or pain somewhere. Today my leg is particularly painful, the usual sciatica; I don't know why I mention it really – you can take it as a given as it is so constant.

My mood is not helped by the fact that no one respects me in this family. I made it clear to Laura that it would be madness to see a therapist, but that is exactly what she has done.

I find out when I'm in the kitchen preparing dinner. Tonight I'm making vegan spaghetti Bolognese, which is a lot of prep and also takes a long time to cook, with constant stirring. Laura comes into the kitchen and drops her bombshell.

Chapter Fifteen

"I know you said I shouldn't talk to anyone, but I felt I was beginning to go mad. As you know, I can't keep secrets, so I have to tell you. I went for a walk just now with a wonderful woman called Jo, and I feel much better already."

I turn off the gas; I don't trust myself not to lose it. I turn around to argue with Laura about the stupidity of seeing a professional. But when I see her happy face looking at me, I feel the anger drain out of me.

"You have to be careful, Laura. Maybe see her a couple more times, since it's making you feel so much better. But whatever you do, don't tell her our plans. And don't let her convince you that Brian isn't a monster."

"There is no danger of that, Henry," says Laura. "From what Jo said today, it seems that she already considers my parents to be awful. And I promise – I will just see her a couple more times, to help get me back on an even keel. And I will never, ever, tell her about our plans."

Just then, George walks in and asks, "What plans?"

"Plans to be free of you," I say. "And your sister."

"Oh. Ha. Ha. Ha. When is dinner ready?"

"In about half an hour," I reply.

"But you know I'm going out soon! Can't it be any quicker?"

As I said. No one respects me in this family.

After dinner, both George and Daisy make swift exits so they can continue with their busy social lives. Laura and I take herbal teas through into the lounge and see if there is anything to watch on TV. There isn't, so I switch it off.

Laura is looking at her phone. "Wow! That is so weird. I have just had a friend request from Lucy."

"Who's Lucy? And I thought you had come off Facebook?"

"I don't look at it much. Lucy is someone I was friends with at junior school. Anyway, I have accepted. Be interesting to see what she is up to."

I pick up the paper to continue with the crossword and Laura turns the TV back on. "You don't mind do you?" she says, "Just whilst you're doing the crossword?"

"As long as it isn't *Love Island*."

"*Love Island* isn't on this year. Well there was one in South Africa, but don't worry, that's finished now. I'll find some old repeat of a living abroad thing to watch ..."

I zone out and concentrate on the crossword for about ten minutes, before Laura says, "Lucy wants to meet up ... She's renting somewhere on the other side of Richmond Park. What a small world! It'll be weird seeing her again."

"So you're going to meet her?"

"Yes, why not?"

"Well just don't go blurting out about your plans to kill your dad."

"Of course I won't. Anyway, Lucy used to really like my dad, strangely."

Chapter Sixteen

Sixteenth sign of a psychopath: ability to be self-deceptive

Laura

Nearly forty-two thousand deaths in the UK. And counting.

Back to the Isle of Wight again, this time with Charlotte. She wants to try cycling around the whole island. This is a crazy idea – the island is so hilly – but Charlotte persuades me to hire electric bikes.

Cycling uphill on an electric bike is a breeze. We collect bikes at ten am from Yarmouth, and return them at five pm, having managed to follow the whole of the round-the-island cycle route, which is around sixty miles. The view along the last stretch of the south coast to Freshwater Bay is breathtaking. Is there another part of the British coast as glorious as this? A long, long bay with the sea looking as blue as the Mediterranean. The ups and downs of the coastal road stretch ahead but hold no fear, as the electric bikes make us look like Tour de France cyclists, we speed up them so fast.

When we get back to Bembridge, exhausted, I wonder how many calories I've burned. Hard to tell, as it seemed so effortless, despite the hours we spent in the saddle. We plan to get a takeaway from the fish and chip shop, but I'm worried that I don't deserve the calories. I try not to ever mention my obsession with calories to Charlotte, as she gets really cross with me about it. I don't blame her; I get cross with myself.

"Just get me some battered haddock, no chips," I say to Charlotte as she heads out.

"Of course you're having chips, I know how your brain is working, always trying to eat less than you need."

So I do have fish and chips and try not to think about the consequences. I only have one large glass of white wine to go with the food, though, rather than my usual two.

I have come to the island not just to be with Charlotte, but to put in place stage one of my plan to kill Dad. Collecting the mushrooms.

Although it is early in the season for mushroom-picking, there have been a few weeks of heavy rain and my research has told me that death cap mushrooms can come earlier after wet weather.

As I push away my empty plate, despite having planned to leave a few chips, I suggest to Charlotte that we go foraging the next morning.

"Yes, the blackberry crop looks huge this year," she says.

"And maybe we could look for mushrooms, too? They were so delicious last time."

"We might be lucky ... Bit early for mushrooms, though. I was thinking if we are looking for mushrooms, we could try and get some magic ones? It's been a long time since we let our hair down ..."

"A long time? I don't think I've even smoked dope since

Chapter Sixteen 105

I was in my twenties. And I have never tried anything like magic mushrooms. You know I don't like to get out of my head."

Charlotte laughs and lifts her wine glass. "So all the alcohol you drink does nothing to you then?"

"I don't drink that much."

"What?" says Charlotte. "I reckon these wine glasses of yours hold a good half bottle!"

It is true – I do like a nice large wine glass. But I don't always fill them right up.

I worry that if I take mushrooms, I might lose control and tell Charlotte all my plans. Henry would never forgive me.

The next day, Charlotte declares, is perfect for our foraging trip. As the mushrooms will be harder to find, she suggests we go up to the Bembridge downs, the same place she found her hoard the last time.

There is a light drizzle in the air and the strong wind seems to make it wetter, as if it is blowing the dampness right into us. We are wearing waterproofs, but my hood keeps blowing away from my head and soon my hair is soaking wet and whipping around my face.

The visibility is not too good, but looking out to sea I can see two container ships in the distance, as well as the Napoleonic fort, which is closest to us here, on what seems to be the top of the world.

Charlotte is ahead of me, and just as I wonder how I can ask her to verify which mushrooms are death caps, she calls me over.

She points downwards. "See these? These are the most poisonous mushrooms. Whatever you do, watch out for these."

I certainly will. After Charlotte has moved on, I go

back to where she has pointed and gather the mushrooms, eight in all. I recognise them anyway; I've been studying pictures of death cap mushrooms for weeks now. I stuff them into one of the small plastic bags I have hidden in my rucksack, which I usually use for collecting up Jeff the Dog's deposits.

That evening, we examine our collection of produce, apart from my mushrooms which I have laid out on newspaper in the bottom of my bedroom wardrobe so they can dry.

We have two large Tupperware containers of blackberries, a saucer holding a small heap of magic mushrooms, and a bowl full of edible mushrooms, which, this time, Charlotte reassures me, do not contain any yellow stainers.

"I'm pleased with all that. Shall we cook some blackberries up to make a compote to go with our ice cream? And then after that, I think it is magic mushroom time!"

"Don't you have to dry the mushrooms?" I ask.

"No, we can eat them as they are."

"I'm not sure I'm really up for this ..."

But Charlotte has her way, and three hours later I feel very strange.

We have eaten about five each, and are watching a video, when I start feeling the effects.

"Maybe we shouldn't have chosen to watch *The Man Who Fell to Earth*," I say. "I feel like I'm an alien myself. I hate to say this, Charlotte, but your face is looking peculiar to me ... I think your eyes are moving to the side of your head ..."

Charlotte starts laughing. And laughing. And laughing. "I can't stop!" she says as tears fall down her face.

Now I'm laughing. "I can't stop either!"

This is not a good time to get a phone call, so when

Chapter Sixteen

Charlotte's phone starts ringing, I say, "Best not to speak to anyone right now."

Charlotte looks down at her screen. "But it's Emily. Why would Emily be calling?" Emily is Charlotte's older sister – I have never liked her, or rather she has made it clear she has never liked me. "I'll have to answer it. I'll try and sound normal."

Next thing I know, Charlotte has dropped the phone and is wailing – extreme loud cries like I have never heard before.

I pick up her phone and hear Emily saying, "Charlotte? Pick up the phone!"

"Charlotte is crying; it's Laura here." I'm doing my best to think straight, but my brain is still scrambling around.

Emily barks at me, like she always has, as though I'm an imbecile. To be fair, I do feel imbecilic right now.

"Listen, Laura, I have just given Charlotte some terrible news. Our father has died."

"Oh my God, I'm so sorry."

"Yes, it's very sad," says Emily, not sounding that sad, "The thing is, you need to look after Charlotte right now. She is obviously in no state to talk to me; she has always been a daddy's girl. When she has stopped screaming, tell her to call me and I will explain exactly what has happened. It's late now, so probably best she calls first thing in the morning when she has had a bit of time to absorb the news. Reassure her there was little suffering. Dad caught a bug a few days ago, nothing serious, we thought, but it took a dramatic turn for the worse this evening and he couldn't breathe. By the time the ambulance arrived, it was too late..."

At this point Emily breaks down herself. So she is human.

"I'm so sorry, Emily, I'll look after Charlotte tonight and she'll call you first thing in the morning."

The awful thing is, the minute I put the phone down, I start laughing and laughing all over again. I'm hysterical. Charlotte is hysterical too, but she is crying and crying.

I manage to blurt out between the laughter tremors: "It is just the shock."

Charlotte looks up at me. She is sitting on the floor, propped against the settee, tears still streaming down her face. She nods to show she understands and then manages to say, "I'm never taking mushrooms ever again."

And that was the end of our little holiday.

The next morning, Charlotte calls Emily to hear all the details. I leave her alone in the kitchen, whilst I go upstairs and start packing.

As I drive home, in between her bouts of sobbing, Charlotte talks about her dad.

I hear the familiar stories about how he used to play with her so patiently when she was little, how he always called her his "cherub", how he encouraged her love of sports and nature.

I always used to love going to Charlotte's house after school, partly because I liked her mum, Susan, and her dad, Peter. Not her sister, who always used to roll her eyes whenever I said anything.

I used to see more of Peter than Susan, as Susan used to work long hours – she had her own small advertising agency in central London. Peter worked in the local council offices and was always home by five-thirty. The first thing he would shout as he came in the door was, "Where are my lovely girls?" And although Charlotte used to sigh dramatically when she heard his voice, she still rushed straight to the hallway to give him a hug. "Aah, there's my cherub,"

Chapter Sixteen

Peter would say as he hugged her. And, "There's my angel", as he hugged Emily.

He was always super nice to me, too. Once he had given his cherub and angel a hug, he would extend his arms a bit wider and say, "Can't miss out Charlotte's best friend. There is room for one more here, Laura!"

At first, I was far too shy to join in, but eventually I would go for the group hug. It would usually end with Emily breaking us up by saying something like, "That's your lot, Dad, we have things to do."

I couldn't help but contrast it with my own dad. He did like a hug on occasion, but it would always involve him making some remark about my size: *"I had better open my arms extra wide to fit all of you in!"*

Right now, my priority is getting Charlotte home in one piece, as she is crying so much, I think she may be getting dehydrated. Once we have driven onto the ferry, Charlotte wants to stay in the car so that no one can see her.

"We can't stay in the car – we aren't allowed. Anyway, we have to wear masks, and that covers up most of your face."

"But I can't blow my nose, and I'll feel like I'm going to suffocate," wails Charlotte.

"Don't worry. We can stand outside, away from everyone."

So that is what we do, with Charlotte gripping onto the rail of the ferry, trying to be brave and look at the horizon without bursting into tears. She fails.

I wonder what is it like to love someone so much? Do I love anyone so much that I would cry like this if I lost them? I didn't shed any tears when Mum died. Do I even have a heart? But then I know without a doubt that I would die for my children. As for Henry, I can't imagine life without him.

Chapter Seventeen

Seventeenth sign of a psychopath: unafraid of consequences

Henry

I was enjoying having the house to myself for a few days, as Daisy has been staying at Ben's and George has gone back up to his student house. But then Laura comes home a couple of days early.

The fact that my heart sinks when Laura calls me to tell me she is coming home, I take as another sign that I'm doing the right thing by leaving this family. Is it just coincidence that as soon as I finished speaking to Laura on the phone, I bit hard into my gum, which means another mouth ulcer will soon be here to torment me?

Laura has a theory that, like my two "philandering friends" as she calls them, a man will never leave a wife unless he has another woman lined up. Well, I'm about to prove her wrong. I have no one else lined up.

The only person I think I could bear to have a relationship with is Charlotte. That didn't work out before, so I

Chapter Seventeen

know I'm deluding myself if I think it could work out again. I wouldn't want to break up her marriage, not that there is any chance she would leave Martin for me. Let's face it, I'm done with relationships. What I would like to line up is not a person, but a place where I can be myself and live a life that properly suits me, and that suits Jeff too.

I have always wanted to live on a houseboat. I would rather have bought a houseboat than this house, all those years back, but Laura was not keen. She said it would be damp. Cramped. Maybe that was true then, but I have been doing some research and you can get amazing houseboats these days. Bright, airy, large double bedrooms, plumbed in bathrooms – some even have Jacuzzis on the deck, not that I would want a Jacuzzi. And they are such great value. You can get a sizeable three-bedroom property for around a third of the price of a similar place on land. And the views are to die for. Who wouldn't want to look out the window while brushing their teeth and see ducks and swans gliding by?

I go houseboat spotting as I cycle along the riverside. When I go on my computer, I never look at human porn; I look at houseboat porn. I have managed to persuade Laura to stay on two houseboats on short breaks away in the last few years – one in Amsterdam and one in Oxford. But they didn't sing to her like they do to me. They left her cold.

This makes it sound like I'm leaving Laura just because she doesn't want to live in a houseboat, which isn't the case. The houseboat symbolises something in a way, as we see our futures too differently. I want a new life, while Laura likes the life she has. There is only one big change she would like to make, which is to get rid of her father.

I have changed and Laura hasn't. One of my main changes is that I have lost all interest in sex. Sex used to be such a driving force for me – it was definitely one of the glues of our marriage. From the moment I first saw Laura in the student union bar, my body reacted to her, as if a switch had been turned on.

And she did turn me on. There is a certain diffidence in the way she moves. She seems to make a slight pause before any movement that gives her a kind of awkward grace that used to get right to me. But now, like the houseboats do to her, she leaves me cold. I have no feelings of animosity, or hatred. She doesn't even annoy me like she used to with her constant inability to make decisions. I simply don't feel anything.

The first feeling to go was lust. The massages we used to give each other that always turned into sex remained just massages. When I held her in my arms at night, I no longer got aroused. We now haven't had sex for around a year. And I don't miss it.

As far as I can tell, Laura doesn't either, as she has never mentioned it. She cuddles me just as much as before, and never seems to even notice that a cuddle always remains a cuddle.

After the first six months of no sex, I did make an attempt to raise the issue. We were alone at our place in Bembridge, in bed. I had my arms wrapped around her, snuggling her from behind, and we had just woken up.

"Do you remember, Laura," I said quietly as my mouth was so close to her ear, "the last time we had sex?"

"It was here, wasn't it?" Laura said. "But it was a while ago now … You never seem in the mood."

Laura turned round to face me and stroked the back of my head. I moved away as her morning breath was not great, and I was worried that mine was probably even worse.

"I don't seem to think about sex anymore, or hardly ever," I said. "Do you miss it?"

Chapter Seventeen

Laura sat up and swung her pyjama-clad legs out of the bed – blue gingham cotton pyjamas, very Doris Day. "I don't think about it either, but I could, if you were up for it?"

"No. I was just checking how you felt about it," I said, but even as I said it, I realised it was a bit pointless to ask Laura how she felt about it. Whenever I ask for an opinion about anything, she often turns it back on me and asks me what my opinion is first.

Which is why I was so taken aback that she decided she needed therapy, even though I had made it clear it would be a mistake. Don't get me wrong – I want her to be her own woman; I have always found it a bit irritating that I end up making all our decisions. I was just surprised, that's all.

Now the fact that I feel disappointed when Laura walks back in the door two days before I'm expecting her makes me feel so sad.

Laura does not pick up on my mood – not surprising, as she has had a lot to deal with. Charlotte never holds back on expressing her feelings, so I can imagine the weeping and wailing that must have gone on in the last twenty-four hours.

It is not Charlotte whom Laura is thinking about, I soon find out, but this woman called Lucy she has mentioned a few times.

I make Laura a coffee, which she drinks at the kitchen table, looking down at her phone. "Lucy has just messaged me – she says she needs to see me urgently. Can we meet for a drink tonight, she asks?"

"I have no problem with you going out tonight," I say. Of course I haven't; I can have a night in on my own. "Why is she so desperate to see you all of a sudden?"

"She says she has something to tell me about my dad ...

Something I may find upsetting, but that there is a reason she needs to tell me as soon as possible, which she will explain."

"All very mysterious ... Brian must have done something awful to her. But why she has to tell you right now ..."

"Well, I guess the sooner I meet her, the sooner I will find out."

"I don't think I need to tell you not to mention our plans to kill the old bastard. Sounds like she might have one of her own!"

Turns out when I meet Lucy that Henry's joke is not that far from the truth.

Chapter Eighteen

Eighteenth sign of a psychopath: detached and cold attitude

Laura

I tell Henry that I will grab something to eat when I'm out, but actually I hope to skip dinner as I have been overeating in the Isle of Wight.

I'm still in a state of shock about Charlotte's dad's dying and I hope to get to the pub before Lucy so that I can have a large drink to help calm my nerves. We have arranged to meet in a pub on Richmond Hill which I can walk to, where Lucy has managed to book us a table. When I enter the bar, I see a woman who looks about the same age as me sitting on her own, looking down. She must be Lucy. Who, I hate to confess to my pettiness, is no longer the slim beauty that was my childhood friend.

I go up to her. "Lucy?" I ask, and when she looks up, I see why she has been hiding her face. She has been crying. She gets to her feet as if to come towards me, but then quickly sits down.

"Oh, Laura! I want to give you a hug ... After all these years."

"Yes, strange times," I say, thanking COVID-19 yet again in my head for saving me from awkward embraces. "Can I get you a drink?"

Lucy gestures to the full glass of what looks like red wine in front of her. "No, I'm fine."

"I'll just get myself something. You sure you don't want something – nuts, crisps, water?"

"No, really, I think you should just get yourself something strong ... I have some shocking news ... God, I feel awful not seeing you for years and then dragging you into all of this. Anyway, get your drink and I can explain."

I find that my hands are trembling as I pay for my drink, a double gin and slimline tonic. I want to run away. It was exhausting being with Charlotte and trying to make the right noises to a woman who loves her father and has lost him, when I so long to lose my own father. And now, I fear, I'm going to have to deal with someone else's pain that I won't understand.

I sit down and wait for the inevitable onslaught.

"I don't know where to begin," says Lucy. Her hands are wrapped around her glass tight. She is wearing seven rings on her fingers, seven golden rings. I don't want to hear whatever she is going to tell me. I count four beer mats on the table. I can see eleven people in all sitting around the four tables near us. There are a hundred and fifty calories in the gin and tonic I'm holding. I remember I have already walked twelve thousand steps today, so I should get up to fifteen thousand ...

"It started when I was seventeen."

Here we go, I think. This is bound to be about Dad trying it on. But it turns out to be more than just that.

Chapter Eighteen

I listen in horror as Lucy describes how she fell in love with my father. Fell in love?

"I met him by chance in a bar. I was with a group of girlfriends – we were all pretending to be older, and your dad was with a couple of other smart men in suits. They all worked together apparently. Anyway, he came over and was really lovely to me, telling me how I had always been his favourite friend of yours and how much he missed seeing me at your house. Then he said he hated to be all fatherly, but should I really be out drinking? He insisted on giving me a lift home. And that was the start of our affair ..."

Lucy takes a big swig from her glass; her hands are shaking more than mine. My mouth must be hanging open in shock, as I'm completely thrown by what she is telling me. I have always known Dad is lecherous, and that he has a taste for younger women, but none of my friends have ever told me that he had come on to them before.

"I can see this is news to you ... I always wondered if you had any idea ..." Lucy says.

"Absolutely none," I manage to say. "We never really saw each other after primary school, though, as you went off to that boarding school. Let me say how sorry I am—"

"It's not your fault. Do you know what a complete bastard your dad is, before I tell you what happened, or will I be shattering everything you thought you knew about him?"

"I'm afraid I know only too well what a nasty man Dad is. But I never knew about you and him ... Again, I'm so sorry."

Lucy barks out a laugh, but it is a laugh that comes from a sad place.

"Again, it's not your fault. It is quite funny really, as you always made it clear you didn't like your dad when we were little, and I could never understand it. Well, I understand it perfectly now."

"So why did you want to meet up to tell me about your affair now?" I ask.

"Oh, it's not the affair that I wanted to tell you about. That was just the beginning of the story. It is what happened at the end. Or rather, *who* happened at the end. It is because of him that I thought I should meet up with you ..."

"Him?"

"My son. Christian. Your father's son. Your half-brother."

Oh. My. God. I don't actually say this because I can't speak. This is too much to take in.

Lucy reaches into her bag and pulls out an envelope. "Here, these are a few pictures of Christian. A few from when he is little, and some more recent ones."

The first few snaps show a small boy around three years old, I would guess, sitting on a beach holding a blue plastic spade. He has Dad's dark colouring, and is smiling happily at the camera. It is obviously sunny, as his eyes are scrunched up.

Then there are some snaps of a man, who looks to be in his thirties. Dark, tall, and wearing a T-shirt and distressed jeans. He is not smiling, as though he is not pleased to have his picture taken.

"Wow, Christian looks great – you must be really proud."

Lucy shakes her head as she reaches to take the pictures from my hand.

"Christian is undeniably handsome. But handsome is as handsome does. I'm afraid he takes after his dad in some

Chapter Eighteen

respects. He lacks any empathy. I love him, absolutely I adore him – he's my son. But proud is not a word I can use."

"I don't know what to say .... I have so many questions."

Lucy sighs. "Of course you do. There is so much to tell you, but I don't think I can answer all your questions now, and after this meeting I'm not sure you will want to see me again, so I will just give you the bare bones.

"My affair with your dad lasted about six months, until I got pregnant. Brian was incensed and wanted me to get rid of the baby. My parents, being good Catholics, were devastated; they wanted me to give up the baby for adoption. I felt like I was being torn in every direction, but that no one was offering to help me, no one wanted to support me. The people I thought loved me seemed to care nothing for my feelings at all. So I ran away."

"Where did you go?"

"As far away as I could. I went to Australia. I had hardly any money, no real plans. But almost as soon as I landed in Sydney, everything fell into place. I got work as a secretary; I met someone who loved me, who really loved me and who looked after me ..."

Lucy reaches into her bag again, this time to pull out a tissue. She blows her nose and dabs her eyes.

"I forgot all about Brian. I had this lovely life in a beautiful city with a gorgeous son and a wonderful husband, Miles. And then everything unravelled when Christian turned sixteen."

Again, Lucy reaches for the tissue as her tears become more overwhelming. For a while she doesn't talk, just mouths "sorry" at me.

It is my turn to say, "There's no need to say sorry, take your time. You have obviously been through a lot."

Lucy barks another laugh of despair before she tries to start talking again.

"It's no good ... I get so upset when I think how perfect everything was ..."

"So what happened when Christian turned sixteen?"

Lucy smiles. "I got pregnant. The day our daughter was born was the happiest day of my life. Miles and I had been trying for a while, and Melanie was the most gorgeous, loved baby. But not loved by Christian. He went off the rails.

"I suppose he was used to being an only child. Once Melanie came along, he became obsessed with the idea that Miles loved her more than he loved him because he wasn't his biological son. He was always asking questions about his 'real' dad. We always said that Miles was his real dad – he was the one who had loved him and brought him up. But Christian grew angrier and angrier, always wanting the fight. He had taken to drinking too, which didn't help ...

"I suppose, considering I had run away when I was young too, that I shouldn't have been surprised when Christian disappeared.

"We spent years looking for him, I even called Brian to see if Christian had been in touch, but Brian told me to never ring him again and that as far as he was concerned, Christian was nothing to do with him, that he didn't believe he was his, as I was such a *slut* when I was younger."

Lucy dabs her eyes again, looking at me with such hurt in her eyes, as though it was me who had said she was a slut.

"I'm sorry my dad said that to you. But why are you telling me all this now?"

"Because the shit is about to hit the fan, and I thought I should warn you. Also, I felt bad, never telling you that you had a half-brother. I wanted to tell you in person, though, and we only landed here a few weeks ago … I should have called or something before, I know, but I kept putting it off when I lived so far away. You and Brian being on the other side of the world, well, it was easy to put you out of my mind.

"Christian got in touch with us about a month ago, told us he is living in London so we flew over right away. We were hoping he had made a great life for himself here."

"And has he?"

"No. Turns out he wanted us over to bail him out. He owes thousands of pounds in rent. He has no job; his drinking meant he was sacked a few months ago from his job working in a pub. I suppose it is ironic that he can't even hold down a bar job. He is staying with us right now – we are staying in an Airbnb in Richmond, costing us a fortune. Lucky Miles is so good with money, or heaven knows what we would do. We are trying to persuade Christian to come home with us."

"You say the shit is about to hit the fan?" I ask. "Why?"

When I hear the answer, I wish I had never asked the question.

Chapter Nineteen

Nineteenth sign of a psychopath: feeling persecuted

Henry

When Laura got home last night, completely worse for wear, I was not in the best mood. I think watching the news on TV had got to me. I feel so trapped in this home anyway, and now with the extra restrictions the government has announced, it feels like the world is closing in.

Yesterday evening Boris Johnson's face infuriated me as he drivelled on about how we need to protect others and his annoying way of hitting the desk with his fist ... When is this going to end? I try and rationalise that everyone is in the same boat, and I write from home anyway, my kids are well, even if their fun is being curtailed at uni. Jeff is happier than ever, he doesn't care ...

Then Laura comes home and delivers another bombshell. So there is yet another horrible relative of hers we have to deal with, an alcoholic monster who wants to bring us all down!

Chapter Nineteen

Once Laura told me the devastating news delivered to her from Lucy, she landed down on the sofa and wailed, "All my life I wanted a brother or sister, but I should have realised that it would have meant yet another awful person in my life to deal with ... Now being an only child seems like a dream. I can't face negotiating with another egomaniac ..."

I sat down next to her, but not too close. I just didn't have it in me to wrap my arms around her to comfort her; I felt so full of adrenalin that I wanted to throw punches, not administer cuddles. I took a few deep breaths.

"Calm down, Laura, we just need to take a step back and think about it rationally. This doesn't change anything for us. This guy ..."

"Christian."

"This guy Christian might be your brother by blood, but you have never even met him. He means nothing to us. And as much as Lucy has all these fears about what he is going to do, well, that could just be a mum worrying too much. That's what mums do ... He hasn't made any effort to contact us, and for all we know he hasn't been in touch with your dad either. Poor guy seems like he is a mess, needs help. Not the type of person who is able to come up with some great scheme to destroy us all ..."

Laura laughed, and then her laughter got a bit out of control. She was soon gasping for air as tears rolled down her face.

"I. Really. Should. Not. Have. Drunk. So. Much."

I went to the kitchen and poured her a large glass of water. When I came back to present it to her, she was a lot more coherent.

"Sorry about that, but you have to admit it is rather funny. I think Lucy was so serious about how the end of the world was about to happen that I got caught up in it. You're right – we haven't heard from Christian, and Dad hasn't said anything and doesn't seem any different from usual, so maybe Lucy is panicking over nothing."

Phew, I thought, Laura was not going to renege on our plan.

We went to bed, and I slept well despite my bad back, but this morning Laura complains that she has hardly slept at all as I hand her a coffee in bed.

"Not surprising, the amount you drank yesterday."

"And the news I was given," adds Laura.

I'm about to ask Laura to go through our plan again, which is to be carried out this week, but she starts crying. What now. I wait for her to explain what is upsetting her – is it the news about her brother? Or the fact the kids have gone back to uni?

No. It is about Charlotte's dad. Really? Haven't we got enough other things to worry about?

Laura reminds me that Charlotte's dad's funeral is today. And how bad she feels about not going.

"He was such a lovely man. And I should be by Charlotte's side – after all she has done for me, these stupid restrictions ..."

"It is a good sign, really. The fact that he has so many people close to him who want to go to the funeral – it would be sadder if Charlotte could fit you in."

Laura sniffs. "I suppose so. I've sent Charlotte a huge care hamper. The awful thing is, I'm just a bit jealous. Why can't my dad just drop down like that?"

"I'm with you there. Would save us a whole lot of bother ... And talking of which ..."

"We don't need to go through it again," Laura says. "I have everything ready. Right now I need to get to work –

I'm a bit behind. I don't know how I'm going to keep a clear head; I feel like it is going to explode." She swings her legs out of the bed. As she stands up, she adds: "Thank God I'm seeing Jo later."

"Jo?" I say.

"The therapist."

And that is when we have what for us is a bad row.

"Really, Laura?" I shout. "Just a few days before you're about to get rid of Brian? You really think it is a good idea?"

Laura then loses her temper and shouts back louder at me: "Do you hear anything I ever tell you? Don't you think things are a bit stressful for me right now? I find out I have a brother, another awful relative, my best friend's dad has just died, our kids have left home … Oh and yes, I have a murder to commit on Saturday! All you care about is me blabbing about our plans, as if I'm some imbecile. I think I have enough other stuff going in my head to talk to Jo about. And hopefully she will be able to calm me down enough so I do go through with the bloody murder …"

I try and defuse things a little with a feeble joke: "Well, if it goes well, there shouldn't be any blood."

But it doesn't do the trick. Laura screams, "Oh ha bloody ha." And stomps out the room, slamming the door behind her.

I sit down on the bed after she has left. I feel winded. Exhausted before the day has even begun. No wonder I have so many mouth ulcers. My tongue probes the two that are bothering me right now. I'm sure one has been there for about two weeks now. Could it be mouth cancer?

Just my luck that the minute I see the light at the end of the tunnel and the chance of having a new life, just me and Jeff, I drop down dead of cancer.

At least I have had some good news, which I haven't

shared with anyone yet, because I was waiting for the right time, which could be a while away now. It is that my agent, Sally, loves the book. It is still too early to worry about what all my friends think of it, and whether they will want to stay as my friends afterwards. Just because Sally loves it doesn't mean a publisher will, after all.

Laura hasn't read my book. She only reads my books after they are published, and even then I can tell she isn't really interested in them, although she always makes out she likes them. Charlotte, on the other hand, always writes thoughtful and long reviews of my books on Amazon.

There is a lot of pretence in our marriage, I think sadly to myself as I decide to stand up and start the day.

Chapter Twenty

Twentieth sign of a psychopath: damaging experiences as a child

Laura

I could do with having a day off, but there is a lot to do, and I have not been able to concentrate lately. The news never gets any better – now forty-two thousand, five hundred deaths have been recorded in the UK due to COVID.

Looking at less depressing statistics, though not good ones, Dave Chapman's business is hanging in there, as his virtual events have brought in enough income to keep him afloat. If the furlough scheme is extended, then fingers crossed he won't have to make any redundancies after all.

Sitting at my desk is a relief – as much as looking at incomes and outgoings is hardly fun, it does switch my mind off from everything else. I think I might go mad if I didn't have spreadsheets to analyse. Then there is my walk with Jo to look forward to.

The weather is still lovely, the last gasp of summer, so

when I do meet up with Jo, all I'm wearing is a summer frock and a light cardigan. This is our fourth meeting, and I'm used to the routine of getting straight into talking almost as soon as we have gone through the gates of Richmond Park.

The park is now noisier as cars are allowed in, plus you have the crazy speeding cyclists to watch out for as you cross the roads. Nevertheless, the trees are still there to remind you that it isn't all bad – the world may be falling apart and people may be catching the virus at a rapidly increasing rate, but the trees in Richmond Park look the same as ever. The temperature is still that of summer, whilst the leaves above us are turning brown, as I comment to Jo, "Time moves on as always – autumn is on its way."

"How do you feel about autumn?" Jo asks me.

Well really, I have rather a lot to get off my chest before I go on about my feelings of autumn, I think. As I have become more confident about speaking what I feel with Jo, that is exactly what I then say.

"So tell me what you want to get off your chest," says Jo obediently.

And I do. Poor Jo, but I supposed that is what her job is, listening to people going on about themselves, never asking her how she is feeling, or if they do, she has to deflect the question back to them. It must be tedious. At least I have some interesting stuff to tell her today, a long-lost brother appearing with evil intentions! Jo echoes my thoughts by saying it sounds rather like a soap opera.

Jo goes on to ask me about my relationship with Henry. She says that I hardly ever mention him, that she has no grasp about what he is like and how he supports me.

"There is nothing to say ..." I start.

Jo chips in: "Ah. I think you will find you do have a lot

to say. He is far more to you than this half-brother you haven't met. So tell me, how happy do you think your marriage is?"

That is the moment I realise that lately, it hasn't been happy at all. I have no idea why not. Although this truth stuns me, I'm too frightened to talk about it. Henry is so adamant that I don't talk about our plans to kill Dad, for obvious reasons, but that is all that holds us together at the moment. Our plans to kill Dad. So how can I talk about my husband?

Wanting to know why I have been quiet for so long, Jo asks what I'm thinking about.

I say that I realise I need to talk to Henry, and that right now, I don't feel like talking about him.

"You know I specialise in couple's therapy? Most people who contact me come for that very reason. I'm sure you must have noticed that was my main focus when you looked me up ..."

"No, not at all," I say. "I just wanted someone I could walk with, rather than be stuck in a room ..."

"You must have looked up other therapists who do walking treatment. I'm not the only one in the area, so why pick me?"

"You were the first one I looked at."

"That might be the case, but you could have looked me up and then moved on when you saw I was a relationship therapist. What I'm getting at is that, from what you have said to me, it seems like you're worried about your relationship with Henry, but that something is making you afraid to go there."

I reply quickly, "Yes, I don't want to go there."

"It is the places we don't want to go to that are often the most important to explore," Jo says. "Do you think Henry would consider coming for a session too – for a couple's counselling session?"

I laugh. "Absolutely not."

"Why not?"

Because he doesn't want to tell you about our plans to kill my father, I think. This therapy business is awfully difficult if you have a big secret you don't want to tell. Perhaps this will be my last session.

When I get home, I find Henry in the lounge watching tennis on the TV (yet again) and tell him that I think I will have to knock therapy on the head.

"Thank God for that," he replies, not looking up.

Then I think about telling Henry that our marriage was the subject that came under Jo's scrutiny today, but it has been a long day and I decide to open a bottle of wine and worry about our marriage another time. After all, I can have at least two glasses tonight – I have only eaten around a thousand calories so far today and my step count has hit twenty thousand. So life isn't so bad, and Henry and I are fine, I'm sure. Jo must assume everyone's marriages are on the rocks, as she sees so many people whose marriages are in trouble.

Just as I sit down in the kitchen cradling the glass of icy, pale rosé, my phone makes its presence felt and Dad's portrait, his latest one, flashes on the screen. I should have found a nicer image to put on my phone, but I suppose any picture of my dad is going to give me a bad turn.

"Hi Dad!" I try to sound chirpy when I answer, otherwise Dad gets angry at me and accuses me of not wanting to speak to him.

"Where you taking me for my birthday?" He screams down the phone.

"I thought you were worried about going out?" I reply

Chapter Twenty

"Not me, I have never been worried about this stupid virus, after all, it hardly affected me. I just didn't fancy leaving the house lately. However, as it is my birthday I thought we should do something special, so you can take me somewhere fancy. None of your second-rate restaurants, I'll leave you to book it. And don't feel you have to bring along that miserable husband of yours."

Well Henry will be so disappointed, I think sarcastically, too frightened to say it sarcastically of course.

Dad's birthday. And the next day should be his death day too, all going well. I might as well treat him to a special meal first, after all, it should also be his last.

Chapter Twenty-One

Twenty first sign of a psychopath: willing to murder for own gain

Laura

So today is the day. Dad's birthday, Thursday 8 October. The COVID death toll in the UK is at forty-three thousand.

Before I leave to pick up Dad, I sit down with Henry and we go through the plan. My present is a book about foraging. I have the poisonous mushrooms mixed into a punnet of ordinary button mushrooms that are part of the shopping I'm dropping off today. In the shopping is also the bacon and eggs. Dad's favourite weekend breakfast is a full fry-up, so he should be cooking the mushrooms tomorrow morning, or at the latest, Sunday.

I was hoping to also take a plastic container full of freshly picked blackberries, to suggest Dad has been collecting blackberries (as well as mushrooms), but although there are still blackberries on the bushes in the Isle of

Chapter Twenty-One

Wight, I haven't spotted any locally, so I can't raise suspicions that the foraging isn't local to Dad's area by leaving blackberries too.

I just have to unpack the shopping, and make sure I give Dad his present before we leave for the restaurant so that I know it will be on display somewhere to be found around the same time he is.

How I will bemoan the fact that the present I gave him – a present that was meant to bring him joy as he loves free food so much – has ended up killing him!

Dad has been going for walks in the woods and fields near his house, and his neighbours know that. He must have been telling Auntie Penny about his walks too, I imagine, as he has certainly been going on about them to me. How a man of eighty-six can walk ten thousand steps in just ninety minutes is impressive. I find it a struggle to do that myself.

Just before I leave, Henry gives me a hug by the front door.

"Gosh, you haven't given me a hug for a while, Henry. You must be feeling all loving because I'm about to do the deed."

"I wish I could be there with you. But I am with you in spirit."

I then say something that surprises me, and certainly surprises Henry.

"Do you still love me, Henry?"

Henry looks like I have slapped him around the face.

"What a strange question. It is our wedding anniversary next week – let's wait until then to get all romantic..."

I had forgotten our anniversary was coming up. And I think it's a big one too, must be thirty years. I'll have to look up what that one means.

"Well, we should have at least one big event to

celebrate, fingers crossed," I say as I pick up all the shopping and present bags I have packed and walk out the door.

* * *

When I get to Dad's I have a terrible pang when I see the effort he has gone to to look smart. He is wearing a dark, pinstripe suit and a jaunty tie, bright pink flowers on a yellow background.

"Nice tie, Dad," I say as I walk in.

"Present from Penny. So, talking of presents ..."

"I'll just put your shopping away, then we can open them in the lounge," I say.

Once we are sitting down, I first pass Dad the presents from Daisy and George, which were actually bought by me. They are two plants, for indoors – orchids from Marks and Spencer.

Dad looks at them briefly, then sighs. "Not very imaginative, your kids." When he opens his present from me, he looks even more disappointed. "A book?"

"I thought you'd like it, Dad – it is about getting free food! Just think of the money you can save!"

"Looks like you're the one who has saved money, buying me such a cheapskate present. Let's hope this restaurant you have booked is a bit special."

The restaurant I have booked is the River Café in Hammersmith, which is way out of my usual price range, but hey, this is a special occasion and should be the last meal I ever buy Dad.

When we walk in, Dad is not impressed.

"This looks more like a canteen than a top restaurant," he remarks. He then gets exercised when he sees the prices

Chapter Twenty-One

on the menu. "Over £40 for a main course? It had better be something outstanding!"

"I think you'll like it, Dad."

The restaurant does have a canteen feel about it – there are no soft furnishings to absorb the noise, so the background chatter is loud. Lucky that Dad has such a big voice. And lucky for the other diners that they probably won't notice his shouting, as there is so much other background noise.

After a surprisingly short chat as we eat our first course, Dad surprises me by asking me about myself. Or, more specifically, about my childhood. Strange.

"I was just thinking about what a weird, miserable child you were," he says. "Was it because you didn't have many friends?"

"I might not have had many friends, but the ones I had were special. I am still great friends with Charlotte. Her father has just died—"

Dad cuts me off with a wave of his hand.

"Oh yes, that loud, big girl. No, I was thinking about when you were younger, before you were ten. Wasn't your only friend that pretty little thing ... What was she called?"

"Lucy?" Dad wanting to talk about Lucy makes me think that she must have been in touch with him. Why would he be steering the conversation around to her otherwise? "Yes, that's the one, Lucy," Dad says, and he has definitely brought the volume of his voice down, to what he would consider a whisper, and most other people would consider normal volume. As this restaurant is so loud, I have to lean in a little closer to hear him. "You ever see Lucy, now?" Dad asks.

"Actually, I went for a drink with her the other day," I say, interested to know how Dad will react.

React, he certainly does. His face goes bright red and he hisses to me, "Well, avoid her from now on! She was always a terrible little liar when she was a little girl, so she is probably even worse now. Stay well clear!"

"How do you know her, Dad? How can you remember that she was a liar? I don't remember her being a liar at all."

The volume of Dad's voice goes up sharply and he does one of his usual table slaps to emphasise his words. "My memory is razor sharp and I never forget a nasty piece of work if I come across one. Always a golden rule for a good businessman: make sure you recognise the vipers. Lucy was definitely a viper. Problem with you is you're a terrible judge of character. Promise me you won't see her again. And if she tries to tell you any stories about her life, remember they are all made up ..."

I should try and calm Dad down by making out that Lucy hasn't told me anything, but I can't resist needling him.

"Lucy did tell me some stories. And you were in them."

I can tell Dad is fuming as so much blood has rushed to his head, I half-expect it to start spurting out of his ears.

"Nothing she has told you is true."

"What do you think she has told me, Dad?" I ask.

"It really doesn't matter what she has told you, as it will all be made up. I'm just giving you some good fatherly advice, and it would be nice if, for once, you listened to me. Now promise me that you won't see or speak to her again!"

I would rather not see Lucy again, to be honest. But I have a feeling that our lives are going to be intertwined whether I like it or not. For now, to keep Dad quiet and to stop him exploding into a thousand pieces in the restaurant, I nod and say, "Of course, Dad. I promise."

Chapter Twenty-One

After all, I don't want to ruin his birthday lunch. His last one ever.

Chapter Twenty-Two

Twenty-second sign of a psychopath: no need for relationships

Henry

As soon as Laura leaves, I fetch Jeff's lead. I need to go for a walk; I can't sit around. Not now.

It is a miserable, drizzly day, but Richmond Park looks spectacular despite the grey skies. The trees are just turning on their autumn display and you can spot stag antlers standing proud of the ferns. I'm careful to keep Jeff on a tight lead, as I don't want a stag to come after him, or me. Can't believe that Laura was stupid enough to almost get killed by a stag earlier in the year.

Laura. Laura. Laura.

When she asked if I still love her, the answer is clear. Of course I do. I must do. It has been over thirty years and we have been through so much together.

But the truth is, my greatest moments of happiness are when I'm on my own, or almost on my own, as there is

Chapter Twenty-Two

always Jeff by my side. With the kids both back at their unis, I'm enjoying having more time on my own. I just don't need people around me anymore.

Laura likes to worry about Daisy and George, and this virus means she has plenty to worry about.

"When will I ever see them again?" she keeps saying.

"Nottingham and Newcastle are probably going in lockdown, so it may be a while ..."

"They might not be home for Christmas!"

"You hate Christmas."

"Because I have to spend it with Dad. But he won't be here this Christmas ..."

"Well, that means we can enjoy Christmas on our own. Or not enjoy. Just forget about it for once – it will be a nice change."

Laura doesn't look convinced and says the words that wind me up so much: "I don't think I can go through with it."

Yet again, I have to sit down with her and explain all the reasons why Brian has to go.

Afterwards I feel grubby. Even I have my doubts about all this. When I think about the alternative, getting the police involved, I can't see how we can avoid dragging Daisy into it. She wants to put it all behind her, bury it. Excavating the past will traumatise her all over again. My resolution has become stronger. I'm doing this for Daisy.

Or rather, Laura is. Right now.

Jeff suddenly drags me off the path, on the trail of some unpleasant scent I imagine. I manage to pull him back. Back on track.

As the path through the stunning beauty of Richmond Park stretches ahead, a vista of autumn glory that is too pretty, too sickeningly pretty to take a photo of, I think of the vista of my future.

Brian should be dead within the next couple of days. Then there will have to be the funeral. A small one (thanks, COVID!). Next, the clearing out of his monstrous home and the sorting out of his finances. Probate. Selling his house.

It will be a lot of work, lots of paperwork, lots of hassle. I reckon everything should be done and dusted within a year. By then Daisy will have graduated, George will be well in to his last year. COVID-19 will not be dominating everything we do (imagine that), as there should be a vaccine.

Looking ahead to a year's time really puts a spring in my step.

I call out to Jeff: "This time next year we will be free!"

I hear a snort behind me. Not a deer, but a young man arm in arm with his girlfriend, who I had not realised were there before.

"Sorry, first sign of madness!" I say to them. "Talking to your dog!"

The man replies, "Don't worry mate. The whole world has gone mad. You're not alone."

We laugh. I can laugh now, but this is going to be a tough year.

As long as Laura is sticking to the plan.

Chapter Twenty-Three

Twenty-third sign of a psychopath: coldness towards others

Laura

After I have dropped Dad off at his home, I sit motionless in the car. What have I done? I'm just about to start the car when my phone calls to me from my handbag on the car seat next to me.

After rummaging around – which is unlike me, as I always leave it in the same pocket, but I suppose things are on my mind – I find it. Charlotte's face is on the screen. I think about not picking up, but decide I need the distraction.

"Hi, Charlotte!"

No reply. I press my ear hard to the phone, and can just about make out a muffled sound.

"You there, Charlotte?"

All I can hear is laboured breathing.

"You okay, Charlotte?"

I realise Charlotte must be weeping, so I wait. "Take

your time," I say, just like my therapist Jo always says to me whenever I break down on our walks.

Eventually Charlotte manages to speak: "It is just that I miss him so much!"

"I am so sorry ... He was a great dad."

Charlotte sounds like she is being strangled as she struggles to take control of her breath. "He was just always there. I know it sounds stupid, but I thought he would always be there for me somehow."

"He is always there, in your thoughts—"

Charlotte then screams down the phone, "Oh! You don't understand. You never understand!" And she slams the phone down, if you can slam down a mobile phone, that is. I imagine that she might have thrown it across the room as she did sound unhinged.

Why is she so angry with me? Is it true, do I never understand?

I think about calling her back but decide she might need some time. I turn the key in the ignition and then my phone calls out to me again. I turn the engine off.

It is Henry.

"How did it go?"

"I'll tell you as soon as I get home; I'm just leaving."

"I'm just going out now," Henry says, "but should be home six-ish."

"Where are you going?"

"Oh nowhere, just having a quick walk with a friend in need."

"Which friend?"

"Look, let's talk when I get home. You must have a lot to tell me ..."

"Yes, bye Henry."

I turn the key in the ignition and this time I manage to

Chapter Twenty-Three

drive off. I'm not looking forward to seeing Henry and the expectant look he will have on his face, his eagerness to hear about how well I have carried through our plan. I want to forget about the whole thing. Again, I ask myself: *What have I done?*

* * *

It is gone seven pm by the time Henry gets home. I'm sitting on the settee in the lounge, not doing anything. I haven't had the energy to pour myself a drink or even switch on the TV. I have just been sitting here for hours.

When I see Henry walk in and the look on his face as he comes towards me, all solicitous, I can't help it. I explode.

"LEAVE ME ALONE!"

Henry puts his hands up and backs away.

"All right, Laura, you have obviously had quite a day. There is a nice bottle of Champagne in the fridge."

"Champagne? This is hardly a time for celebration!"

"I'm sorry, I thought you would need a drink – it just seemed after all our hard work to get to this day, we should mark it."

I do need to drink. I stand up, march into the kitchen, and fling open the fridge, grabbing the Champagne bottle. Turning to Henry who has followed me, I say, "Okay, get the glasses then."

We sit down at the kitchen table and my first two glasses are gone within minutes.

"You ready to tell me about how it went?" asks Henry.

"No," I bark. "But I'm ready for another glass of this."

Before we know it, and although we are drinking in silence, we have got through another bottle of wine. I begin to talk and find I can't stop. I tell Henry everything, well almost everything. He should look delighted, but he looks sick.

He reaches for my hand across the table.

"What have we done?"

I stand up and go and get another bottle. The wine doesn't take away the bad feelings, but it helps us through the next couple of hours.

Until we start being sick. We only have one bathroom, but do have one other separate toilet, which I lurch to, whilst Henry heads for the bathroom. I don't know how long I'm cradling the cold ceramic bowl, but I stay there until the words "Ideal Standard" printed on the inside of the toilet bowl become clear and I'm able to stagger up.

I check to see if Henry is still in the bathroom, but he is gone. I weave a painful path to the kitchen. I fill a tumbler full of water, which I gulp down in one. I then fill the glass again. I would fill another glass for Henry, but I know I won't be able to carry two glasses to the bedroom. It is like walking on a ship in stormy seas as I make my way up the stairs. Henry is unconscious on top of the bedclothes, snoring loudly. I collapse onto the bed next to him.

Before the spinning room slows down and I edge into sleep myself, I ask myself, yet again: *What have I done?*

And the answer soon comes: *Not enough.*

Chapter Twenty-Four

Twenty-fourth sign of a psychopath: manipulative behaviour

Henry

I have never welcomed a hangover before, but it is a relief to feel so ill that my head is fuzzy. I don't want to think clearly, I can't face where my thoughts may take me.

It is also a relief not to be able to talk when you can't face a conversation. Laura looks grey as I cook us a fried breakfast. I place her plate down in front of her, and say, "Let's hope your dad is having a breakfast like this right now."

Laura grunts. I think I should shut up. So I do.

Naturally, Jeff has no idea what is going on, so he expects his doggy needs to be met as usual. Today's walk in the park is a struggle. Apart from my still feeling ill, horrible thoughts are trying to make themselves felt in my fuzzy head. I do my best not to let them in.

"Murderer!" the rustle of the leaves seems to be saying. "Murderer!"

I look away from my feet and up to the horizon framed by the colours of dying leaves on all the trees. Amazing how blood red some of the leaves are.

We got so drunk last night ... I remember we did lots of talking; in fact, we talked more than we have done in years. I try to remember what we were talking about. Anything apart from what Laura had done that day at Brian's house. Now that I think about it, she deliberately avoided telling me anything at all. Was she hiding something? She is terrible at lying and hiding the truth from me, but I was so inebriated I would not have been able to read her as well as I usually can.

The more I think about it, the more I suspect that Laura is hiding something. And then I know. She has not gone through with the plan.

The leaves stop telling me I am a murderer and instead make normal leafy sounds.

Rather than feeling enraged, I realise I feel relieved. Of course Laura wouldn't be able to kill her dad. What were we thinking? Some madness must have overtaken us; there is always a better way to move forward than committing murder and risking getting caught. What seemed like a brilliant plan to get rid of Brian now seems like the most ridiculous, idiotic, and downright crazy thing to have considered.

I fish in my pocket for my phone to call Laura. To tell her I know, and that everything will be alright.

I feel almost euphoric ... Thank God she hasn't gone through with it.

Laura answers and before I can speak, she says, "Can't talk, I'm with Charlotte." And puts the phone down before I can say anything.

Chapter Twenty-Four

I hope that Charlotte does not tell Laura what happened yesterday. I should have told Laura I saw Charlotte, that we met at the river in the early evening, but I was so confused afterwards. I didn't know what to say, and then we got drunk and I was too incapable to say anything.

When I get home, I decide I will cook a celebratory meal. This time I will not open any wine; I will not let alcohol take over. We will talk properly. We will work out how to cut Brian out of our lives for good, in a sensible way. Everything is going to fall into place.

Laura walks in just as I'm chopping up aubergines. I'm singing along to that earworm of a Pharrell song, "Happy".

The look on Laura's face is a picture. "What the hell?" she says, and then she laughs ... But not a happy laugh. A laugh empty of joy. Pharrell's song runs out of energy.

"I know I was murdering that song," I say, "but there is no need to give me that look and then laugh at me."

And then Laura sits down and bursts into tears.

"Is this about your dad?" I ask.

"No," sniffs Laura, "I have been dumped. After all these years." She stops speaking as tears overtake her again. I wait for her to recover enough to continue.

"Charlotte told me I'm a psychopath. She says she suspected that I deliberately tried to kill my dad when George went to see him when he probably had COVID. Now that her own dad has died of COVID, she realises just how evil I am. it was a complete revelation, she said – she feels stupid not to have seen it before.

"She added that she now realises I have no feelings, that it has always been her that has put the effort into our friendship. She said that now she is the one who needs support, I am like a stone, completely devoid of sympathy. It is obvious I have no understanding of what she is going through. And she is right! I don't have any idea! I have never felt anything like she does. Not only do I not love my own dad, I tried to kill him! How can I possibly relate to her situation?"

As I listen, I wonder if I have contributed to the end of the friendship. When I was with Charlotte yesterday, did I say anything that could have led to this? Does the fact that she turned to me in her hour of need mean that she now sees me as more than a friend? That she can't therefore bear to see Laura anymore, as she has feelings for me?

I try and remember exactly what Charlotte said to me yesterday. There wasn't much talking, because Charlotte was crying on a bench when I met her, and mostly cried all the time we were together. I did put my arms around her to comfort her – was I imagining that Charlotte was hugging me back a little too hard? Or was it me who was holding her too tightly?

Before I can think of what I should say to Laura, a phone rings loudly. Her phone. I have always hated the ringtone she uses – it is such a loud abrasive one. I must suggest she changes it. I hear her say: "Dad?" And then shout, "Dad? ... Dad? Are you okay?" Laura doesn't speak for a while, just presses the phone hard against her head as though she is trying to hear something very faint.

She looks at me, her eyes wide with fear, still pressing her phone to her ear. Then she lowers the phone slowly. Her mouth is open, but no words are coming out.

"What is it, Laura, what did he say?"

Laura suddenly moves as if she has been given an electric shock and reaches for her bag she has put on the kitchen table.

"We have to go," she says. "I think Dad is dying."

Oh. So I was wrong. She did go through with it.

Neither of us speaks as I drive us to Brian's house. I turn

on the radio at one point, but Laura reaches straight out and turns it off.

When we get to the house, we both continue to sit in silence in the car. But we can't stay like that, so I say, "Right, let's go!" Which sounds ridiculous, but at least it gets us moving.

The daylight is just fading and Brian's front garden is eerily quiet.

I take the keys out of Laura's trembling hands and we enter the house, which feels empty of life. I know what I am going to find and steel myself. Laura collapses on the stairs whilst I take a look around.

Nobody. Or rather, no body.

Upstairs, I first go into Brian's bedroom. The bed is unmade, but otherwise there is nothing to see there. I then try the door of his en-suite. Locked. One large shove is all it takes for the door to give – either I'm stronger than I think, or Brian has a terribly ineffective lock on the door. The door swings open and bangs loudly into the wall whilst I take in the sight of Brian lying motionless on the floor.

He is wearing a smart, cream tracksuit – good quality, you can just tell even if it didn't have the Ralph Lauren logo to prove the point. Only the best for Brian. The bottoms are around his ankles and he is lying curled up on his side next to the toilet, as though he toppled over whilst sitting there. His head rests next to the bath with its tasteless gold-plated taps in the shape of dolphins. Near him on the floor is his mobile phone, face down, so I can't see its screen. There is no blood, or any other bodily fluids. It is all rather clean and savoury. If only Brian's tracksuit bottoms were pulled up, it would be a very dignified looking death. That is, if he *is* dead.

I feel a cold wave go through me. I want to turn around

and walk out. But I need to make sure. I lean over him and place my palm near his nose and mouth. Is that a faint breath I feel on my hands, or am I imagining it? I grab some toilet tissue from the gold-plated dispenser and bunch it in my hand. I then place this over Brian's mouth and nose, holding it tight and pinching his nostrils. I wait for what I estimate to be two minutes before I take my hand away. I remove the tissue and hold my palm near Brian's mouth and nose again. Nothing. If there was breath before, I'm sure there is none now. I stuff the tissue in my pocket.

Whether or not Brian was breathing before makes no difference. Even if he was dead before I got here, I have still killed him. It is because of me that he is lying here on the bathroom floor.

I am not a good man. I am a murderer.

Chapter Twenty-Five

Twenty-fifth sign of a psychopath: faking emotions

Laura

Soon after we get home, the phone calls begin. I have to tell everyone that Dad is dead, and then react appropriately when they give me their sympathies. Sympathies I do not deserve because I'm happy. I have been monitoring my emotions, thinking that maybe I'm secretly devastated that Dad is dead, but I'm not. I'm relieved. I always thought that Dad was a burden to me, that his presence made me miserable, but that maybe I would realise that I actually loved him when he died. But now he is dead, I know I never loved him. I'm relieved he is dead. Happy, even.

A large part of my feelings of relief are because it wasn't me who killed him. I never went through with the plan. When I told Henry that I never put the poisonous mushrooms in Dad's fridge, that I threw them away, to say he looked startled is an understatement.

I told him as soon as we arrived home, after finding Dad's body.

Henry had poured us both very strong gin and tonics, and we were sitting in the kitchen.

"I can't believe it," I said. "I just can't believe it."

"That our plan worked?"

"But it didn't work, Henry. I never went through with it."

"Don't fuck with me, Laura." Henry looked sick.

"I'm not!" I said. "Did you really believe I could kill him, truly believe it? Me?"

"No, I was just thinking on my walk today that of course you wouldn't be able to finish off your dad. But the evidence points to the contrary."

"It is a bit of a coincidence," I agree. "But Dad was getting very worked up when I went out for lunch with him. He looked like he was a heart attack about to happen. He always said he had that heart attack in New York – you know that sordid story he likes, sorry, liked to tell which involved cocaine and prostitutes ..."

"What were you talking about at lunch then?" asks Henry.

"We were talking about Lucy. I think she must have been in touch with him. I think the shock of Lucy coming back into his life, and his son that he doesn't want to acknowledge, was stressing him out. I think it's something to do with Lucy and Christian that has frightened him to death. Literally."

Our kids seem underwhelmed by the news, but I expect it will hit them later – or rather, hit Daisy, as she has been so damaged by Dad. They both ask if they are expected to come to the funeral and whether they are even allowed to come. Which I reassured them that they are.

Chapter Twenty-Five

I'm glad that Daisy seems pleased that she had an excuse to come home, as I think the funeral might help her find some sort of closure. George complains that coming home would mess up his studies, as he probably wouldn't be able to get back to Newcastle due to all the restrictions. He loves that house he is renting and the friends he is living with, so I say he doesn't have to come to the funeral if he doesn't want to.

Next, I call Auntie Penny. She bursts into loud sobs as soon as I give her the news. "He was a complete bastard," she eventually says between bouts of crying. "But I loved him. He has been there my whole life ... I can't believe it."

I decide now is not the time to tell her that all he has left her is the watercolour of her as a baby; I don't want to make her cry even more.

After calling his cleaner, Teresa, and his gardener, Jacub, I think it is time to call Lucy.

As soon as I tell her, Lucy wants to know how I found him and when I found him. She asks lots of detailed questions: "Did the house look very different? Did it look like there had been a fight? Are you sure he wasn't stabbed?"

"Stabbed?" I ask, shocked. "He definitely was not stabbed – there was no blood. Why on earth do you think he might have been stabbed?"

"Oh, thank God," says Lucy. "I think you should know I had a fight with Christian earlier today – he insisted on getting your dad's address off me. He said he was going to go and get your dad to pay him back for the way he has been treating me, and the fact that he can't recognise his own son. He was going to sort him out, he said. Sort him out! I was terrified he was going over there to kill him. I begged him not to go!"

"Have you seen Christian since?"

"Yes, he came back later this afternoon. Said it was all sorted. When I asked what he meant, he said: 'You'll soon find out.'" I was terrified he had done something terrible, and now your father is dead.

Could Christian have killed Dad? Surely if he had somehow despatched him, there would be some sort of sign of a struggle or something? I suppose an inquest will show what Dad has died of.

Maybe he was murdered by one of his children, after all...

I promise Lucy that I will go back to the house and check there is nothing untoward there. Yet another chore to add to my list.

Somehow, when something big like this happens, you expect other demands on you will stop.

But this week, as well as sorting out stuff to do with Dad's death, which involves a huge list of things to do and calls to make, I have to see Dave Chapman, have a smear test, and oh yes, it is our anniversary.

I turn to Henry who is next to me on the sofa. "Can we forget about our anniversary this week?"

"Fine by me, it's forgotten," he says – a little too quickly and eagerly, to be honest, but at least it removes something from my to-do list.

"And I want to check on Dad's house, see if there is any sign that Christian was there ..."

In the morning, after an almost indecently large breakfast, we decide that we will get the trip to Dad's house over with first. The drive there is very different from the last one we made. This time we both sing along to the radio as we drive. I notice that Henry really puts his heart into it when "I Want to Break Free" by Queen comes on. I hope that

Chapter Twenty-Five

isn't some sort of sign. Sometimes I think Henry can't stand living with us all anymore.

At Dad's house, I head into the study, whilst Henry stays in the kitchen, emptying the fridge of anything that could go off soon.

On top of the desk is Dad's will. Strange. He never left it on the top. I pick it up and call Henry.

"Look at this!" I say when he comes into the room.

Henry reads the first few paragraphs.

"We have to get rid of this," says Henry as he passes it back to me.

"We can't! Dad was always going on about his will. Auntie Penny will think it strange if there isn't one."

"Check in his filing cabinet – see if there is an old one there."

I do, and I find the will that I recognise and remember. I leave it in its place.

The will that I have just found on the desk has obviously been left by Christian. I decide that it is only fair to remove it, as it would throw a heap of suspicion on Christian if I left it there. That is the excuse I tell myself for taking it home. Nothing to do with the fact that the will says: "*I leave all my worldly goods to my son, Christian ...*"

Whilst Henry drives home, I examine the will. It has got a wobbly, illegible signature at the end. Doesn't look like Dad's usual signature at all.

"So this is what killed Dad. Christian must have paid him a visit and made him sign this. Dad still is, sorry, was a big guy, so Christian must have had a knife or some sort of weapon to threaten him with. No wonder Dad had a heart attack."

"There must be witness signatures on the will," says Henry. "Who else has signed it?"

"People I have never heard of."

"Then we are doing Christian a big favour by taking the will away. It would only look bad for him if we left it there."

I don't think Christian will see it as a big favour, though. Which, of course, he doesn't.

Chapter Twenty-Six

Twenty-sixth sign of a psychopath: blaming others for own actions

Henry

Today is the day of Brian's funeral, three weeks after his death. As I sit in the crematorium, I can't believe that this is all happening so smoothly. The post-mortem showed Brian died of a heart attack. There were a lot of steroids in his system, which might have contributed. I told Laura I suspected he was taking steroids, but she never believed me. Not that we would have been able (or willing) to do anything about it anyway. There are no suspicious circumstances as far as the police are concerned. No one is going to be accused of his murder.

In my opinion, Brian died by his own hand. Apart from being so vain that he took steroids to build muscle, if he had acknowledged his own son like he should have, the shock of seeing Christian wouldn't have been a shock at all.

Our area going into tier-two lockdown ten days ago

meant we had to have a very fraught meeting with Lucy and Christian outdoors to sort things out. Though maybe that was a good thing in the end. I reckon if we had met indoors, Christian might have ended up stabbing someone. Even though we were in the middle of the park, things were touch and go.

Laura called Lucy straight after we had been to check on her dad's house and had found the will. We arranged to meet with Lucy and Christian at the gates of Richmond Park a week later, on the first Saturday after tier-two restrictions had come into force, which meant we were no longer allowed to meet indoors, which, as I said, was just as well.

Laura and I took Jeff as he loves the park, and I suggested it might make things more friendly, somehow, having a dog there. He did break the ice with Christian, who, despite everything I had heard about him, was charming. At first.

As soon as we arrived at the gates, we spotted Lucy, in a large leopard-print coat that swamped her, standing next to a man who had the air of a rock star, with the dark glasses he was wearing adding to the impression that he might be someone famous. Lucy waved at us, and we went over. Laura introduced me, and Lucy apologised that her husband couldn't make it, but introduced Christian who was making a huge fuss of Jeff, which Jeff was lapping up, or rather leaping up. He was on his hind legs with his paws on Christian's thighs whilst his tail wagged furiously.

"Down, Jeff!" I said, but Christian laughed and said he loved dogs and didn't mind at all.

Then Christian turned to Laura.

"You must be Laura, my sister. Shame I can't hug you – this is not how I wanted my first meeting with my big sister to go ... I want to ask you so much about my dad, our dad ..."

Chapter Twenty-Six

Laura gave a weak smile. "I can't believe I have a brother. It is a shame we are meeting this way, but let's hope that in time we can get to know each other in a more normal way."

I heard Lucy give a loud, laboured sigh. A sigh that suggested Laura and Christian were never likely to have a normal relationship.

We all walked a little way into the park, and despite the dampness of the weather, sat down on a bench. Lucy and I at the ends, Christian and Laura next to each other in the middle. No room for social distancing.

Laura reached into her bag and pulled out the will, handing it to Christian.

"Yours, I believe."

Christian stopped being charming. He spat out the words: "Our father signed that – it is what he wanted."

I answered on Laura's behalf, putting up my hands in what was supposed to be a calming gesture. "Before we decide whether we can use this will or not, why don't you talk us about this signature of Brian's which is nothing like his usual signature? And also, how you got the witness signatures."

"Never mind the signatures, it is what Dad wanted!" shouted Christian.

"Just talk us through what happened when you last saw Brian," I said. "There's no need to shout. We just want to know what happened. We can talk about the will's validity afterwards."

"Who are you, the police?"

Suddenly things got scary because Christian pulled out his hand from his jacket pocket to show that he was holding a knife. He stood up and faced us with the knife pointing at me, making it clear it was me he wanted to fight. It was only a small blade, but when you have a knife pointed at you, the fear is indescribable, no matter what type of knife it is. Before my bowels betrayed me, Christian put his hand back in his pocket, turned around, and started walking away.

Lucy called him back. "Come on, Christian, we are on your side. We are family." And then she found the right words to call him back: "You aren't going to get a penny if you walk off now."

Christian turned round.

"But throw that knife away before you come anywhere near us," Lucy said. "You half scared me to death with your stupid showing off."

Christian threw the knife into the undergrowth and came back, but stayed standing, looking down at us. I wanted to stand up too, but didn't trust my legs to support me.

"I just want what is rightfully mine!" Christian said.

"My inheritance as well as yours?" asked Laura.

Christian sighed. "I suppose it was greedy to put myself down as sole heir. But otherwise, I get nothing."

"Sit back down," Lucy said, "and let's talk about it. I'm sure Laura and Henry can meet you halfway."

I stayed silent. It seemed to me that Christian didn't deserve a penny of Brian's money. Laura was the one who had had to put up with her dad for all these years, who'd had to bear the brunt of his nastiness. It was obvious that Christian was hardly going to do anything useful if he suddenly came into some money. Piss it up the wall probably. Buy more knives with it to threaten people with.

As if Lucy had read my thoughts, she continued: "You have hardly shown yourself to be someone Laura and Henry are likely to trust with any money, Christian. I suggest we talk things through, and maybe find a way for

Chapter Twenty-Six

you to get your fair share in a way that makes everyone happy."

"You mean tie up some money in some way?" asked Laura.

"You're an accountant, Laura, I'm sure you can think of some solution."

By the time we left the park, we weren't exactly all friends, but we had definitely come to some agreement that meant I was no longer worried that Christian was going to come to our house in the night and threaten us with a knife, like he had with Brian.

Christian gave us the bare bones of what had happened the afternoon of Brian's death. He had surprised Brian at home. He said Brian didn't want to let him, in, but that Christian forced his way inside. Brian ran upstairs and shut himself in the bathroom.

Christian hammered on the door and Brian screamed at him to go away, that he was calling the police. But he didn't call the police; he must have been calling Laura, we realised. Then Christian said he heard a crash, which sounded like Brian had fallen over. Then silence.

The silence went on and on. Christian thought about breaking open the door, but instead decided to leave. First, he had faked Brian's signature and put the will he had brought on the study desk. He wiped down the outside of the bathroom door and hoovered the hallway before going, as he wanted no trace of his visit. Which seems ridiculous to me, when he had left that incriminating large piece of evidence on the desk.

And now he sits about four rows behind me, as if butter wouldn't melt in his mouth.

I turn around to see who else is here. Not a bad turn out – there must be the full thirty you're allowed. Brian would have been horrified that it was such a small number; he would have expected hundreds of weeping acolytes to turn up.

No one is weeping. Not a moist eye in the house as far as I can tell. Even Teresa, his loyal cleaner, looks quite chirpy. I expect Brian told her she would be well looked after should he die before her; I also imagine it didn't occur to him she would outlive him. He used to laugh about her, how much older she looked than her "mere" sixty-odd years. I make a note to self to make sure we give her a sizeable thank you gift once all the money is sorted out. She deserves it.

I have no idea who most of the people here are. And I will never know, because we have a good excuse for not having a wake afterwards. Thank you again, COVID.

After a summary of Brian's early years and his career in the City by the celebrant, whom I am convinced Brian would have approved of, as she is tall, slim and attractive (not that I'm rating her in such a trivial way myself, of course), Laura walks up to the lectern at the front of the chapel and begins her speech.

"I'm so happy to be standing here. At last. I thought my dad might outlive me and I would never get the chance to tell you all what a nasty, selfish monster he was. I have no happy stories to tell of a doting father – just stories of a man who liked to bully, belittle, and manipulate his only child. I got off lightly, though. Other women, particularly young, vulnerable women, suffered far more. He got immense pleasure – sexual pleasure – from preying on the innocent. He got one of my school friends pregnant when she was just seventeen. Worst for us, he molested our daughter, more than once. They are not the only ones who have been traumatised by Dad. I'm sure there are many people now who are still suffering from post-traumatic stress disorder after having been in contact with him. Destroying people was a fun hobby as far as Dad was concerned.

"Another favourite past-time of Dad's was exploiting people. I see many of you here who spent time helping him out because you are kind people. Some people take advantage of kind actions such as yours. Dad was one of those people. I hope you never get manipulated by such a horrible person again.

"The good news is that we are free of Dad now. The bad news is that he got away with it. He was never made accountable for his actions, and for that I'm very sorry."

This is the speech I hear, because this is the speech that Laura wrote and read to just me at home, the speech that she wanted to give. But, after a lifetime of being worn down by Brian, it was a speech she did not have the strength to deliver, and I can't blame her for that. I don't have the courage to tell the truth at the funeral either. All that Laura actually does is thank everyone who has come and also thank them for all their kind actions during Brian's life.

As we troop out to the sound of Elgar's *Nimrod*, I have another tune playing in my head, "I Am Free" by New Life. I almost hum it out loud: "*I am free to run, I am free to run, I am free to dance ...*"

I walk outside with a positive spring in my step – that is, until I feel a horrible twinge in my left leg. No matter how good things may get, no matter what new life I make for myself, I will still be living in this body that is falling apart. Wherever I go, I will have to take my ailments with me.

Chapter Twenty-Seven

Twenty-seventh sign of a psychopath: unable to read other people

Laura

With everything that is going on, you would think I would be stressed about probate, about sorting out Dad's house, about Christian. Not to mention that George is stuck in Newcastle which seems to be just about the epicentre of the pandemic. Plus, the COVID death toll is now forty-six thousand in the UK and rising fast.

But you know what is bothering me the most? The smear test I have just had. It was agony.

The nurse who did it said it was because I have gone through the menopause, so it was my fault, not because of her rough treatment of that torture equipment she put inside me.

I searched on the internet afterwards. I have vaginal atrophy. After looking at what I can do, I realise I need to talk to Henry. About sex. This is a subject we never discuss.

Chapter Twenty-Seven

We never used to talk about it because we just used to get on with it, quite often. When we suddenly stopped doing it, there was nothing to talk about anyway.

I think maybe the breakfast table is not the place to bring it up. I then choose not to talk about it during the day. After all, I have a lot to do. I have decided to give up work; I can't fit it in as well as sorting out probate. Plus, I won't need the money anymore. I have been resigning my handful of clients one by one over email, but I think it is only fair to tell my longest-standing client, Dave Chapman, in person. I have arranged to meet up with him for coffee this afternoon. Despite all the restrictions, it is fine for us to meet up in a café, apparently.

Dave has chosen a place in Teddington, near where he lives, which means I have to drive there. It is a real problem finding somewhere to park, as the town is heaving. Eventually I do find somewhere and then am further stressed when I walk into the café to see that it is choc-a-block too.

Everyone is out. I'm not sure this is really in the spirit of the current restrictions. Surely not everyone in this café either lives together or is having a business meeting? My suspicions are confirmed when I earwig on the conversation of the two women at the next table. They are discussing some teacher at the school both their kids go to. She is rubbish apparently. So be warned, if you live in Teddington and your kids have a teacher called Mrs Waterson, they aren't going to learn anything!

My attention is drawn back to Dave, when he suddenly reaches out and grabs my hand. What is going on? I quickly withdraw it and say in what I hope is a jokey manner: "Don't you know there is a pandemic on, Dave? What you doing – trying to infect me?"

"I'm so sorry," Dave says. "I don't know what came over

me. Knowing you mustn't touch someone just makes the desire even stronger, don't you find, Laura?"

I decide there needs to be a bucket of cold water poured over this conversation immediately. "No," I say rather more loudly than I intended. The two women at the next table turn their heads to look.

"I just wanted to comfort you, Laura," Dave continues, "as your father has passed away. It was a natural instinct."

That is when I make Dave cry. Not intentionally. After I tell him that I will no longer be working for him, he breaks down. Who knew that my services meant that much to him?

He looks down and only the slight shudder of his shoulders gives away the fact that he is either crying or laughing. I give him time to compose himself, resisting the temptation to reach out and touch his hand to comfort him. I don't want him getting the wrong idea.

Too late, he has the wrong idea anyway. We end up having an extremely awkward conversation where I find out I have somehow been giving Dave the impression that I don't just care about his business, but about him – personally. Apparently, from the few things I have said about my family life (and honestly, I can't remember saying anything at all), I have given the impression that I'm in a loveless marriage.

I think that, as Dave has been on his own so much lately, he has added up two and two to get five. A mistake that I, as a numbers person, would never make. It is horrible to let someone down, but I have no option. Saying goodbye is never easy, but the look on Dave's face when I say goodbye and leave makes me feel particularly awful.

Chapter Twenty-Eight

Twenty-eighth sign of a psychopath: abusive behaviour

Henry

Tonight, Laura says she wants to talk. Daisy has gone back to Nottingham; she says it is more fun in her student house, which is hardly surprising – we are hardly a bag of laughs here. So it is just the two of us. There is nothing stopping us talking, to tell the truth.

Except, I'm not ready to talk. I'm not ready to tell Laura that I'm leaving. That I have feelings for Charlotte, that I now dare hope may be reciprocated. Nothing is certain yet, and I don't want to hurt Laura until I know exactly what my plans are. Until I know exactly how much pain I will be inflicting.

As usual I do the cooking, whilst as usual Laura hits the wine, drinking two glasses before we have even sat down to eat. Not that I'm counting – it is Laura who always insists on telling me exactly how much she has drunk all the time;

she has an obsession with adding up her alcohol units each week.

"I had better not have any more," she says as I go to pour some more wine into her glass, "I have already had my twenty-four units this week."

"Twenty-four? I thought your limit was twenty?"

"In usual times, yes. But these are not usual times."

"So what do you want to talk to me about?"

"I think it is more of a sitting-down-on-the-sofa conversation."

Oh dear, has Laura guessed what I'm feeling, what I'm planning? But no, I soon find out she really hasn't.

After dinner, sitting side by side on the settee, Laura at last spills the beans. She tells me all about her smear test and that the only "cure" for her is if we start having regular sex.

"That hardly puts me in the mood," I say.

"I'm sorry, Henry, I don't know what to do."

Then Laura tells me some news that does get me in a mood, if not *the* mood.

She tells me about her earlier meeting with Dave Chapman. The oily bastard, I have never liked him. Not that I ever met him, but she dropped his name into conversations far more often than is necessary. She never mentions her other clients.

I feel rage spread up from my toes to my head. I don't know why I'm so angry. I should be pleased; I should be trying to encourage this relationship. So why has this news riled me?

I'm not angry with Laura; I trust that she hasn't encouraged him. But I feel tempted to jump in the car, drive round to Dave's house and punch him.

"So where does Dave live?" I say.

Chapter Twenty-Eight

Laura laughs. "What you going to do, drive over and hit him?"

"Of course not!" I lie.

When we go to bed, Laura reaches over and holds my hand. Something stirs within me, I'm not sure exactly what. I'm certainly in no mood for love-making, but it is nice to hold hands.

I release my hand from Laura's and turn over. "Goodnight."

"I love you, Henry," says Laura, which just about breaks my heart.

"I love you, too, I mumble, before pretending to fall asleep.

When I'm sure Laura is asleep (which isn't hard to know, as she snores quite loudly), I get up and go to the study.

I switch on the computer. I need some distraction so I go to YouTube. The video I click on is a music video in which the singer Ingar van Calkar looks stunning, although not as gorgeous as the two dogs she is walking. I consider whether it is a real fur coat she is wearing whilst the words of her song echo my confusion: "*Hold You. Hate You. Love You. Leave You.*"

I simply don't know whether I want to leave anymore. The minute Laura told me about slimy Dave trying to get his hands on her, my gut reaction surprised me. I couldn't stand the idea of anyone else having Laura; I still can't. It was as if a blade of truth came down and sliced through a blindfold I didn't know I was wearing.

I still want to be with Laura. I don't want anyone else. The fantasy I have been having about Charlotte ... What was that all about?

All the planning I have been doing in this last crazy

year, I now see was a form of escape from what I couldn't bear to see. I was in such a painful situation when Brian was alive that I failed to see what was right in front of me. I just wanted to escape from here, from everyone. The real issue was my own feelings of helplessness that I could not help Daisy. I also blamed Laura for what happened too, as though it was her fault.

If anyone is to blame, it's me. I need to battle my own demons before I do anything too drastic. I just hope I have the strength to do it without putting any blindfolds back on. Sometimes the dark can be so comforting.

I'm about to go back to bed when I hear a knock on the door. At this time? I go downstairs and can make out the shape of someone through the frosted glass. "Hello?" I call out.

A familiar voice replies, "Just open up!"

I open the door and then before I can say anything, I'm floored by a hard blow. I think it was aimed at my head but I managed to duck so that it landed on my shoulder.

"What the hell?"

"Do you want to come outside, Henry, or are we going to do this here?" Martin says, his voice low and controlled.

I don't want Laura to hear anything, assuming she is still asleep, so I step outside, shutting the door behind me, which is stupid as I don't have a key on me.

Martin is standing a few feet down the front path now, and in the darkness he looks even bigger than in the daylight. I don't want to be hit by him again – I'm still in a lot of pain from the punch to the shoulder.

"You bastard," Martin spits out. "You absolute bastard," he says again, just in case I hadn't got it the first time.

I put my hands up (Ouch! Is my shoulder broken?). "What's this all about?"

Chapter Twenty-Eight

"You tell me," Martin says.

"Let's go for a walk around the block, I don't know what you think I've done, but whatever it is, it can't be as bad as you think."

Every step, my shoulder warns me that I have probably sustained permanent damage.

As we get further away from the house, Martin's voice gets louder: "I thought you were a friend. But friends don't move in on your wife, especially when she is feeling as vulnerable as Charlotte is right now."

"Has Charlotte told you I made a move on her? Because I swear to you I haven't."

"Oh, you don't fool me with your 'I'm such a good friend, I'm just going to comfort you' act, and you didn't fool Charlotte either. She was so shocked after your little talk by the river when you groped her that she didn't know what to think. She was so surprised that at first she kept it to herself, in case she had made some mistake. Then tonight she told me everything. She said she no longer wants to see you, or Laura, ever again, as you have both let her down so much. Her closest friends in the world! How could you?"

I'm stunned. I know I thought that our embrace by the river could be misinterpreted – I misinterpreted it myself – but I honestly thought it was Charlotte clinging on to me, not the other way round. I'm not quite sure what to say, as I don't want to make out Charlotte was encouraging me in any way, but before I can say anything, Martin turns to me.

"You know what, forget it. Whatever lying excuse you're about to give me, you can keep to yourself. All that matters is that we never want to see you again. You and Laura are dead to Charlotte and me. So steer clear of us; we will certainly be steering clear of you."

Exit Martin, as he marches to the car.

Which leaves me and my extremely painful shoulder stuck outside.

So much for turning over a new leaf with Laura; I'm going to have to lie about all this. I knock and knock and knock on our front door. Thank goodness Jeff starts barking his head off, or I don't think Laura would ever have woken up.

She lets me in.

"What are you doing outside?"

"I just wanted a quick breath of fresh air. I couldn't sleep, and I forgot my keys."

"And you forgot to put some proper shoes on too," Laura chuckles. "Fancy going out in your slippers. I hope you didn't go far in those pyjamas – people will think you have gone mad." She nudges me playfully on my shoulder.

I scream.

"You okay? have you hurt yourself?"

"I fell over on the footpath. I suppose these slippers are well named ..."

"You want me to drive you to A&E?"

"No, I'll put some ice on it, and go in the morning if it's still bad."

But it isn't my shoulder that feels bad in the morning; it is me. I'm so ashamed of my behaviour. I'm sure I used to be a decent man. Can I become one again?

Chapter Twenty-Nine

Twenty-ninth sign of a psychopath: love of money

Laura

Another lockdown – not surprising with the number of COVID deaths escalating so fast. The total is now over forty-eight thousand. Everything is so different from when the country shut down the first time. I drive over to Dad's house and get stuck in traffic, which is a complete contrast from Lockdown One when the roads were lovely and quiet. Where is everyone going? Eventually, I let myself into the eerily quiet house and sit at Dad's desk. Time to start the massive job of going through his papers and sorting out his stuff.

On top of my list for today is ending his mobile phone contract. I take out Dad's mobile phone and switch it on. It buzzes to let me know there are messages and missed calls. I open up the messages and the first one I read, from someone called Julia, sends a chill through me. It is all in caps.

"WHERE IS THE MONEY?"

I scroll down the messages and see there are lots in a similar vein, not all from this Julia.

I compose one response for all text messages and emails saying: *"Mr Brian Maxwell died on 9th October. You can reach his solicitor, Geoffrey Melville, at Geoffrey.Melville@melvilleandco.org."*

Thinking about it, I should phone Geoffrey myself. He was at the funeral, and when he shook my hand in his usual creepy way, he had said that I must get in touch with him as soon as I was able, before starting on probate.

When I get through to Geoffrey, after a bit of a fight with the receptionist who wants to check that I'm a worthy enough caller, there follows an awkward conversation that becomes surreal and then dumbfounding. Why can't solicitors just say things outright? It takes me a while to cotton on to what Geoffrey is telling me. But then, it would be a lot to take in, no matter how it is worded.

I first find out that all the shares and savings accounts that Dad was always showing me are no longer. Geoffrey says that Dad sold all his shares and emptied his bank and savings accounts over the last few years.

So where has all the money gone?

There is a lot of prevarication from Geoffrey on this point. He says there are many "claimants" on Dad's money, but now that he has died, these demands should stop. But, he warns me, I should be prepared for some rather nasty stories appearing in the press.

"So was Dad being blackmailed in order to stop stories appearing in the papers, Geoff?" I ask.

"Geoffrey, not Geoff please," says Geoffrey. "Ahem ... I'm not sure I would exactly call it blackmail; just let's say your father had many obligations that he had to discharge."

Chapter Twenty-Nine

I take that as a yes; Dad was definitely being blackmailed.

Geoffrey goes on. "Laura, you shouldn't really have gone to your father's house without consulting me ..."

"Sorry?"

"But whilst you're there, you will find the latest will your dad wrote in the drawer of his desk. I believe he always kept it locked. You will find the key taped behind his last portrait. Do you want me to wait whilst you read it?"

"Oh, this is all very dramatic," I say. "Yes, please hold on a minute."

The key is exactly where Geoffrey says and I find just one piece of paper lying in the drawer. Usually, the wills Dad showed me were a few pages long, but this piece of paper clearly states *Last Will and Testament* at the top.

I read the first line. I reread it.

"Have you found the will, Laura?" asks Geoffrey.

"Yes."

"I wouldn't bother reading through it all – not that it is very long – as you will not find your name anywhere on it. I expect this must come as something of a shock to you, as I know Brian didn't like to admit to anyone that he was effectively broke. I was happy to help out, as his friend, and take on his debts. That is why he has left everything to me.

"I hate to be brutal, but you're trespassing on my property right now. I would be grateful if you would leave your set of keys on the dining room table before you vacate. Please feel free to take any small keepsake you like, but I'm aware of all the items of value in the house, and these will be needed to pay off any debts. Please make sure to leave your father's mobile phone, too. I may need that to reach certain of his contacts."

Geoffrey ends the call with a curt "Goodbye". Not even "Goodbye, Laura".

Sick is too mild a word for how I feel. I slide off my chair, fall to my knees, and then lie down on my side on the beige office carpet. At first, I think I might faint. My body is bathed in sweat and I feel hot, but I stay conscious. My thoughts are not coherent; there is a fire burning in my head.

Eventually, a calmness descends and I manage to sit up.

All those times I had to sit in this room, being watched by Dad's portraits whilst he went through that charade of making out I was going to get all his money. Of which, according to Geoffrey, there isn't any. Not that I trust him any more than I did my dad. Those two horrible men were cut from the same cloth. Geoffrey must have had some awful hold over Dad to be made the sole beneficiary. He was probably the biggest blackmailer of Dad out of all of them.

I shouldn't be surprised that Dad lied to me.

As the more rational side of my brain takes control, I tell myself what Geoffrey has relayed to me is good news. I'm now completely free; I never have to set foot in this vile house ever again.

I am distressed that there are people out there who have been so hurt by Dad that they felt compelled to come after him. And what about all the people who were never brave enough to say anything to anyone?

I hope there are stories in the paper. I want Dad's crimes to be exposed. I just hope it helps some of his victims, including Daisy, to heal.

I don't want any keepsake to remind me of any of this place, although I do pick up the watercolour of Auntie

Chapter Twenty-Nine

Penny on my way out. Looks like she is the only relative who is getting anything from Dad's estate, even though it is something she probably doesn't want.

I sit in the car and slowly count to ten, and then ten again, before I drive away for good.

Epilogue
October 2021

Henry

Life on a houseboat is everything I could ever have imagined, maybe even better. Every morning I take my coffee outside onto the deck and watch the swans sail by. There is an awning I can sit under when it rains, so it is my joyful morning ritual to contemplate life on the river no matter what the weather. Jeff loves it, too, though we are trying to train him to stop jumping into the river to swim after the ducks.

This morning is one of those splendid, sunny mornings that promises an unseasonably warm October day. I won't dwell on the fact that this is thanks to global warming; I don't want to ruin my mood. My health has never been better. Apart from the occasional twinge here and there of course, but then I am almost sixty, so I should expect some wear and tear.

At my age I should have known better than to have acted the way I did over lockdown. As a father I was absent. As a husband, well I am lucky that Laura has stuck with me.

I now see that my actions, let alone my thoughts, were close to unforgivable. Not only did Laura have to put up with an abusive father, but with a partner who failed to give her the love she deserved. I was disloyal and controlling. I thank my lucky stars that Laura has managed to forgive me and start afresh.

The last year has been one of recalibrating, recovering, and resetting

Recalibrating has been a matter of rewiring my brain in every way. I'm so glad I came to understand that I could not throw away all that we had together. I realise now that it wasn't Laura I wanted to leave; I was desperate to escape my situation, what with Brian's nastiness seeping into our lives, tainting them. Lockdown on top of it all made me – made us all – feel so trapped. These aren't excuses for the way I acted, but explanations.

Recovery is still a work in progress. Clearing my head has been no easy task, and getting over that year and a half during which COVID was king and Brian died has been hard. We are having to work at things. Laura persuaded me to go to counselling with Jo, and those walks in the park, the three of us together, are healing. I will never again scorn the idea of counselling.

Seeing her parents turn to a professional has encouraged Daisy that it isn't such a bad idea to get some help, and she has been seeing someone, too. She never talks about it, though, and we don't ask. She has been intruded upon enough by her relatives.

I think a few stories in the papers about Brian have been of some comfort to Daisy, knowing she is not alone. Brian would be incensed to know that he never made front-page news, just a few paragraphs where you could easily miss them. He would be even more infuriated to think that he spent all that money on his two blackmailers, when the damage they could do in the media was so trifling. Mind you, to Brian, his reputation, his image, his status was everything.

Reading the stories of the two women in the papers was more proof (not that we needed any) that Brian got immense gratification from hurting people. Both women were just starting their careers in the same firm as Brian at the time he took advantage of them. I hope the money he gave them and telling their stories in print has helped their recoveries.

Resetting has been the easiest part of our new lives, as it means making plans and having hope. Laura and I spent many hours after the shocking news about the will, thinking about ways of rejigging our finances, working out how we could live more simply so that Laura could give up work. We eventually decided that if we let out our place in Richmond and rented somewhere for ourselves that was further out of London and much cheaper, we could live well, with the earnings from my surprisingly generous book deal topping us up.

We should easily have enough to live comfortably until our pensions, that Laura was wise enough to set up, kick in.

Christian was predictably livid when he found out there was no inheritance. He tried to come after us for money, and we had to call the police in the end when he tried to break into our house in the middle of the night. I don't think there is any hope of a sister-brother relationship forming. We are all relieved he is back in Australia now, with plenty of distance between us.

I think Jo enjoys hearing about all the dramas of our family life, although she is always the epitome of cool and collected. Her counselling has helped Laura and me to work out the dynamics of our relationship, about giving each

Epilogue

other space and listening to each other, properly listening. Jo talks about co-dependency a lot; it seems to be all the rage and we are right on trend.

Laura offered to give river life a try, as she knew it meant so much to me as well as it making solid financial sense. Her fears that it would be damp have been unfounded, so far at least. We don't have a hull, as this is more of a house on a floating platform than a boat, so that helps.

Laura's other reservations have proved unfounded, too. She thought the kids would rebel, but they have taken to the boat much better than either of us expected. Turns out it is a brilliant venue for parties, now that we are allowed to have them again.

In fact, Daisy is having a "gathering" tonight – just ten people she promises – so I can only hope she means no more than twenty. She seems to be partying a great deal, but then, after last year, who isn't? Daisy has plenty to celebrate, too – she got a first and then landed a job in the city, no mean feat for a graduate right now. George is also happier, now that he gets to experience (almost) proper university life with most restrictions over.

To get out of Daisy's way, Laura and I are going to Charlotte and Martin's for the evening. Our relationship with Charlotte and Martin, for all of us, has taken extra hard work.

It was Charlotte who made the first move towards reconciliation – she texted Laura about a month ago, suggesting they go for a walk.

I texted Martin soon after, suggesting that we go for a walk too. I was amazed that he said yes.

I don't think he is completely convinced that I never had designs on Charlotte, and let's face it, he is right – I did have some designs. But I have convinced Martin that I'm determined to do everything to make my marriage work, and that I would never do anything stupid to jeopardise it.

"I can't forgive you mate," he said. "I can't forget either. But your and Laura's friendship means a lot to Charlotte, so I'm prepared to move forward and put it all behind us. They were emotional times, last year, after all. But if you ever try anything like that again, you won't just be dead to me. You will be properly dead."

I think the counselling, combined with Brian's death, has helped Laura to be more open. She now talks about stuff she would never have mentioned before. It can be too much sometimes, to be honest. I'm not sure I need to know about everything I do that makes her feel "undervalued", for example. Why can't crockery be left to drain on the draining board overnight? For goodness sake!

After half an hour of nature watch on the deck, I go inside and make Laura her coffee.

When I go into our rather minimalist bedroom – everything is all white, from the paintwork to the bedding – to hand Laura her coffee, I find she isn't there; she has already got up. I can hear her in the shower, singing. One of the ways that Laura fills her time now is having singing lessons and she has joined a local choir. As I listen to her loud rendition of Here Comes the Sun by the Beatles, I try and be pleased that she is singing instead of noticing that she is murdering the song. I then consider joining Laura in the shower. But, although our sex life has come back to life to some degree, we tend to plan things rather than be spontaneous. We both take a lot more warming up than we used to.

I bend down to put Laura's coffee on the bedside table when I feel it, a sharp stabbing in my shoulder. I shouldn't have moved so quickly when I put down the mug as any sudden movement can set off the pain. Then I hear a loud splash and realise Jeff must have jumped in the river again.

Life. Honestly, just when you think you're getting it sorted, it reminds you that you never will. I slowly straighten up and walk crookedly back out to the deck.

"Jeff! Jeff!" I call out but he is on a mission. The ducks are far too clever for him, though, and he has no chance of catching one. I ease myself down onto my chair and allow myself the luxury of watching our dog splashing around making an idiot of himself. I know exactly how he feels.

Acknowledgments

I wrote this novel during lockdown, so thanks to everyone in my family who helped me through that, my husband Julian and our children Lyra and Ellis, who unlike the student children in this novel are a constant delight. And that is said without any motherly bias. Kathryn Price, as always, helped me beyond words, but particularly with words. Thanks also to my supportive editor Claire Strombeck and to Alex Beach for his eagle eye and useful input. Special thanks to Matt Broadhead for his understanding of grammar shared with me years ago when we worked at Marketing Week, but which I've largely forgotten.

Cover and book formatting by Peter and Caroline O'Connor from BespokeAuthor.

Printed in Great Britain
by Amazon